FLIGHT LU-365

AF127762

Marie A. Rebelle

Flight LU-365

Uitgeverij Aspekt

FLIGHT LU-365

© 2016 Uitgeverij ASPEKT
© Marie A. Rebelle

Amersfoortsestraat 27, 3769 AD Soesterberg, Nederland
info@uitgeverijaspekt.nl - http://www.uitgeverijaspekt.nl

Cover design: Maurice Hof
Inside design: Sosan Hanifi

ISBN: 9789461539441
NUR: 455

All rights reserved. No part of this book may be reproduced, stored in a retrieval system, or transmitted in any form or by any means, electronic, electrostatic, magnetic tape, mechanical, photocopying, recording or otherwise, without the written permission of the publisher: Uitgeverij Aspekt, Amersfoortseweg 27, 3769 AD Soesterberg, Nederland.

Printed and bound by CPI Group (UK) Ltd, Croydon, CR0 4YY

Flight LU-365

Marie A. Rebelle

This is a work of fiction. Names, characters, businesses, places, events and incidents are either the product of the author's imagination or used in a fictitious manner. Any resemblance to actual persons, living or dead, or actual events is purely coincidental.

Acknowledgements

A special thanks to:

C.P. McClennan for writing the lovely and endearing foreword for my book;
'Honey', Michael Knight and **Rye** for taking the time to beta read my manuscript;
Patricia, Liza and **Leonora** for believing in me and always encouraging me;
Maurice Hof for creating the beautiful and striking cover for my book.

Last, but definitely the most important:
My husband, for always supporting me, giving me the time to write and pursue my many dreams, for encouraging me and believing in me, for loving me. I could not have done this without *you*, my love. Thank you!

~ *Marie Rebelle*

Foreword

It was a dark and stormy… pffft… who am I kidding.

It wasn't stormy at all. It was dark, though, but it was unseasonably warm in March of 2014 as we entered a pizzeria in Bristol, England.

Yeah, a pizzeria… in Bristol… who knew?

It was already a very confusing and whirlwind day for my wife and I. We had just flown in from Toronto and driven across from London after eloping the day prior.

Into the pizzeria we trudge, and being in England, the word trudge fits being we Canadians were confused by the warm temperatures as we attempted to kick non-existent snow off our boots simply out of habit.

We sit down at our table and I come eye-to-eye with this redhead. You know the one I'm talking about.

The one that grabs your mind, wraps it around her little finger and then toys with it until you're looking for cigarettes. And I don't smoke, so that's saying something.

Marie Rebelle sat across from me at that table. A woman that was already a great friend to me even though this was our first face-to-face meeting.

I cannot recall exactly when we became friends or even started talking, but it had been at least a couple of years before we finally met in Bristol. I was already a fan of hers having watched her site evolve with constantly new fiction, blogging, and photos that caught the eye and provoked thoughts.

Being you are holding this book, her words have evolved again, but we'll come back to this.

She had been blogging, at least, a year prior to my starting my Stranded site, so I looked to her for advice and assistance. And she did assist while becoming one of my biggest writing supporters, a confident, and even a muse for a story or two that I have written.

Now, I said we would come back to the book you are holding, and I recall hearing how excited she was first telling me about this work. She honoured me with a request to beta read for her.

An adventure ensued, however, and I have a new appreciation for editors. Being the initial manuscript was not written on an English-language computer, it was difficult trying to deal with a word processor that marked everything in red and claiming it was all wrong.

That word processor has serious psychological issues and sulked for many days as I trudged through

(TRUDGED!) and told it that Marie's words were, in fact, correct. I don't think that word processor likes me anymore. I believe it now makes up errors on my own work just so it will feel better about itself.

I'm sorry, I digress...

More recently, Marie honoured me again in asking me to write this little ditty that you are currently reading.

This story you hold now was shocking to me as I read through it. Having read much of Marie's erotica, I knew she had writing chops. The subject of a plane crash, however, is so outside of what I would have seen as her first novel. It has reminded me of the old iceberg metaphor in that we don't have full visions of our online friends and acquaintances, but only that small peak that sticks above the cybersea. People forget how multifaceted the human experience is, even if we don't see everything.

And in the story of a plane crash, how can we see everything?

I don't want to distract you any further from the reason you bought this book... and if you didn't buy it but stole, or pirated this... shame on you.

PUT IT BACK!

In closing, I am so proud for Marie that she has been able to succeed with this book. She sunk a lot of time, sweat, and ink into what you are holding. More so, as with all her blogging and writing, she has given you a little window into herself.

My wife and I look forward to our next visit with Marie and her husband. It may not happen in a Bristol pizzeria again, but it will be an adventure.

Ooooh… maybe an Irish pub in Morocco!

C.P. McClennan
Author of Darwin's Sword – Savannah Book Two
Mississauga, Ontario, Canada
January 23, 2016

Tribute

This book is a tribute to all victims of airplane crashes.

I could have written a book in any genre: drama, thriller or a reflection of the facts of one of the many airplane crashes that put a black border around aviation history. However, I chose to write a book in the erotic genre. This does *not* mean I have no understanding of how horrendous and sad airplane crashes are and the impact it has. In fact, this story reflects something of my mind. It reflects my own fears; my fear of being ripped from this life before I have done all the things I still want to do; before I have experienced all the wonderful things we have planned; before I have reached my goals; before I have traveled the world with my husband. Sometimes, the thought of not being able to do it all, frightens me to the point of pure panic.

My goal with this book is to show that people who died in plane crashes were more than just a photo and a couple of words. in a newspaper. They had loved ones and friends, different jobs, different backgrounds and different preferences in the ways they lived.

They had a *life*.

The inspiration for this book came in the weeks after Malaysia Airlines flight MH17 crashed on 17 July 2014. That day 298 people died and 193 of them were Dutch.

The 298 who perished

Malaysia Airlines' passenger list shows flight MH17 was carrying 193 Dutch nationals (including one with dual US nationality), 43 Malaysians (including 15 crew), 27 Australians, 12 Indonesians and 10 Britons (including one with dual South African citizenship).

There were also four Germans, four Belgians, three Filipinos, one Canadian and one New Zealander on board.

At least six of those killed were delegates on their way to an international conference on AIDS in Melbourne, Australia.

Professor Joep Lange – a prominent scientist and a former president of the International AIDS Society (IAS), was among those who died.

His colleagues have described him as "a great clinical scientist" and "a wonderful person and a great professional".

Other stories of passengers and crew emerging include a Malaysia-Dutch family of five, a Dutch couple on their way to Bali, an Australian pathologist and his

> *wife returning from a European holiday, as well as a Malaysian flight steward whose wife – who also works for Malaysia Airlines – had narrowly escaped death when she pulled out of a shift working on missing flight MH370.*
>
> *Source:*
> *http://www.bbc.com/news/world-europe-28357880*

The Netherlands played a big role in the recovery of the bodies. I sat glued to the television screen to see the ceremonies as the bodies returned. It moved me to tears when I thought of the people who lost their loved ones in this horrible act of terror. I couldn't imagine the way in which the crash would change their lives. Suddenly, everything was different. All plans they had made were off the table. I could almost feel their pain. My tears were also for the victims. They were torn from life so abruptly. They had no notion that their plans for the next day, the next week, the next month would never be executed.

I was proud to see the way my country handled this, the dignity and respect with which they treated each victim of the crash. They placed every person in a separate coffin and transported the coffins from Eindhoven Airport to Hilversum in separate hearses. This symbolized a way to give each victim back their individuality instead of grouping them under the header 'victims of flight MH17'. Just like back in 2001 with the attacks on 11 September, I followed the news. I searched for articles on the internet. I read everything I could find about the victims of this crash – the grandfather who traveled back home with his grandkids, the young couple who were going on holiday, who wanted to be married, the owners of a well-known restaurant, entire families gone – mother, father and kids. I still feel a lump in my throat when I think of all those people around the world who had been touched by this terrible tragedy, as well as by other tragic plane crashes.

The idea to write this story took months to form in my head. It's not the story of MH17. I will leave it to others to write about the facts surrounding that horrendous act of terror.

This is a story about a plane crash, focusing on the lives of the victims, not their deaths.

This book is *my* tribute to all victims of airplane crashes.

~ *Marie A. Rebelle*

Prologue

"No! No! No! No!" the man in seat 12C chanted. People cried and moaned. They screamed. Some were in a near catatonic state, not making any sound. Panic stifled the air. Worse than the panic was the whining screech of the engines.

Only minutes before, the plane was quietly flying at cruising speed. People read books and magazines, slept behind the airline blindfolds, talked or listened to music. Each passenger tried to make the long intercontinental flight as comfortable as possible for themselves. Some members of the flight staff tended to the needs of passengers while other attendants cleaned away the last remnants of the dinner they had served. In the cockpit the pilot and the co-pilot kept their eyes on the instruments, while the plane cruised along on auto-pilot. Nothing warned of a pending disaster.

Two loud bangs shook the plane and ended the peace on board. Immediately the nose of the aircraft pointed downwards. In the cockpit, the pilot switched to manual control of the plane while both he and the co-pilot scanned the different dials on the instrument panel for a sign of the problem. Confusion had the upper hand. According to the instruments everything was in order and the plane was still level on ten thousand feet. Reality was different. The plane was in a steep dive towards the earth below.

The cabin manager called the cockpit from the back of the plane.

"What's going on?" the purser asked, trying to keep the panic out of his voice.

"No idea yet," the co-pilot answered. "Any signs of problems from where you are?"

"Nothing. No fire, no visible damage to the wings or engines."

"Will get back to you!" the co-pilot said and broke off the connection.

In the meantime, the pilot had sent out an SOS distress signal to the nearest international airport, which was Windhoek in Namibia. With nothing abnormal showing up on the instruments, the pilot couldn't tell the traffic control officer in Windhoek what problem they faced.

While the pilot and co-pilot followed the emergency procedures, flight attendants tried their best to move up and down the aisles, holding onto the seats to steady themselves. They instructed the passengers to put their heads between their knees and brace for impact. Oxygen masks didn't drop from their storage compartments as the cabin pressure was still okay, but also because the instruments in the cockpit didn't register any emergency. Children cried as their parents panicked. Parents comforted their children while a mortal fear gripped their hearts. Couples held hands, whispering assurances and loving words to each other and expressing regrets about not having the life together that they had imagined for themselves. People who traveled alone sent thoughts to their loved ones at home. Some prayed. Others cried. Some were silent and others screamed.

"No! No! No! No!" the man in seat 12C still chanted while hugging his knees and shaking his head from side to side.

"Please Lord, make it quick," an older woman in 28E prayed.

"Mommy, what's happening?" a four-year-old boy asked, but his mother just held him tighter while tears silently ran down her cheeks.

"Now I will never get to meet him," a woman in 37A whispered.

"I love you," one woman said to the woman next to her. Their heads were between their knees but each had one arm around the other. They had their eyes locked for eternity.

The end came less than ten minutes after the panic started. Up to the point of impact the pilot tried to get the aircraft level and to gain altitude again. All attempts failed. The yellowish brown sand of the desert below raced towards them. The co-pilot held his arms in front of his face, not able to watch his own death approaching. The pilot hung back in his chair, pulling on the yoke with his full weight. In the cabin, flight attendants still tried to calm passengers, ignoring their own panic. They had trained for this. The loud whining sound of the engines mixed with the moans, the cries and the screams.

Impact ended every sound.

Silence.

Silence, except for the crackle of fire.

No more cries. No more panic. No more prayers.

The neat rows in which the passengers sat were now a chaos of metal, bodies and luggage. Briefcases and bags spilled out their contents. Papers lifted and flew away on the gentle ocean breeze. Sounds of small explosions replaced the silence in the quiet desert. The front part of the plane had slid up and stopped at the top of a dune, etching the nose and wings against the darkening sky. The waves of the cold Atlantic Ocean gently brushed against the intact tailpiece of the aircraft. Twisted steel, damaged suitcases and broken bodies covered the road which ran parallel to the coast and right through the disaster site. In this remote area of Namibia, somewhere between Swakopmund and Walvis Bay, no one had witnessed the crash.

The night came quick in the Namib desert. It was like someone had switched off a light – one moment there was daylight, the next moment it was pitch-dark. Only the small fires burning in the wreckage gave an eerie shimmer of light. About half an hour after the plane had crashed, the first flashing blue and red lights approached the remote disaster site from both sides. Flight traffic control informed the emergency services in both Swakopmund and Walvis Bay of a possible crash in the desert when the plane disappeared from radar in Windhoek. They gave the coordinates where the plane might have crashed, not knowing whether it disappeared into the sea or crashed in the desert. In Windhoek a delegation of officials and investigators boarded a small aircraft to take them to the crash site.

Not one passenger or crew member of Flight LU-365 noticed the new noise around them. Sounds of sirens filled the air as the emergency vehicles came closer. Even after the noises had died down, the desert held its breath. Nature was dark and quiet.

Waiting.

Blue and red lights of police cars couldn't reveal the horror that the dark of the desert hid away from the people who spilled from the insides of the vehicles. Emergency procedures started. The first priority was to look for survivors.

They found none.

Chapter One
Cathy

Cathy looked around at the mess in her bedroom. Clothes were everywhere, scattered across the floor, on the bed and over the chair in the corner. The doors to the closet stood wide open, as did the drawers of the dresser on the other side of her room.

"How am I ever going to decide which clothes to take with me," she mumbled.

She didn't really expect an answer to this question. Cathy lived alone, but it was not by choice. She was single, in her early thirties and more than ready to be in a relationship. For years she had tried everything to meet 'Mr. Right', but nothing worked out the way she hoped. Cathy glanced at the desk behind her and smiled when she saw her laptop. She had found her 'Mr. Right'. Her thoughts wandered back to other ways she had tried. She remembered several dinners with friends. They invited single men to join the dinners and tried to hook her up with them. Each time she was glad when she got home again. After that followed a period in which she went out to bars to meet men, but she only met the creepy ones. She smiled at the memory of her desperation when she told her friend she would walk her dog every Sunday. Cathy had hoped she would meet men in the park.

"Do you want a dog?" her friend asked.

Cathy fiercely shook her head.

"So, if you meet someone, what should he do with his dog?" was her friend's next question.

Needless to say, Cathy never walked her friend's dog.

Cathy shrugged and returned her attention to the mess in front of her. She needed to get her suitcase packed, but it was still empty.

"Maybe a cup of tea will help," she said and walked to the door of the bedroom. She stopped halfway towards the door and glanced at her laptop again.

"No, Cathy," she said, "not tonight!"

It was still early, but with her alarm set to wake her up in the wee hours of the morning, there would be no online time tonight.

In the kitchen she switched on the kettle and put a big mug on the counter. She made herself a peanut butter sandwich while she waited for the water to boil. Minutes later she sat on the couch, eating the sandwich and slowly sipping her hot tea. She was right about the tea, or at least about taking a break from the mess in her room. Tea had always been her remedy when her mind was in chaos and this time it helped too. While she sipped her tea, she organized her thoughts and as she organized her thoughts, it became clear what she should pack. As soon as her cup was empty, she walked back to the kitchen, rinsed the cup and the plate and put it away. On her way back to the bedroom, she thought about her life.

Cathy came from wealthy parents and had moved in middle-class social circles from a young age. About two years ago she had enough of the snobbish attitudes in those circles. Men pretended to be the perfect husbands while they fucked around with their wives' best friends and women constantly visited spa retreats for treatments they believed kept them young. Cathy never seemed to fit in with the others. She was always the odd one out. She went to a spa retreat with her mother and three of her mother's friends on two occasions, but both times it bored her after the first hour. Cathy preferred to stay busy. She didn't like spending her days under tanning lights or having her nails painted or her feet massaged. It was not even the activities as such that bored her, but the endless tea-drinking, together with the senseless chatter and the compulsory afternoon naps. Her mom was upset when Cathy declined to join them a third time, but Cathy refused to change her mind.

Being of middle-class parents had its benefits. Cathy received a superb education. Her parents had opted to enroll her in a private school, which only the 'rich kids' attended. It was nothing different from a normal school, except that her parents had to pay a huge sum each year for her tuition. Mean kids were everywhere, no matter their parentage. There was no question whether Cathy would go to university, because money was never a problem. She studied Business Administration, but didn't stop after she had her Bachelor's degree. There was no need for her to start work just yet, so she continued studying for three more years until she had her Master's degree where she specialized in international marketing. Only then she looked for a job. Her father wanted her to take a job in his company, but again she went against the norm of the higher-class and refused. She landed a job with another company where she started at the bottom of the corporate ladder. Cathy worked hard to get herself to where she was now: head of a small marketing department. She loved her job, and she was good at it.

The only thing in which Cathy saw herself as unsuccessful, was finding a life partner. This was much to the despair of her mother who couldn't wait to see her daughter – her only child – in an extravagantly expensive wedding dress. Cathy knew that would bring on the next disappointment for her mother, because she wanted something simple and classic. She didn't share her mother's love for earthly goods and lust for status. Her mother had tried many times to introduce her to unmarried men during huge dinner parties held at her parents' house, but without success. Cathy's taste in men differed hugely from that of her mother. All the men at her parents' dinner parties worked for her father. They all hoped to marry the boss's daughter and climb the career ladder quicker than their peers. This disgusted Cathy to the point where she often declined her mother's dinner invitations, claiming that she had to work.

She found peace in herself when she stopped going to the dinner parties, or tried to be hooked up with single men by her friends. Cathy concentrated on her work, went out on a frequent basis and connected with people on social media. The last thing she looked for online was a relationship. It was just a way to unwind after work – a way for her to meet people outside the closed circles in which she had been moving.

It happened when she least expected it. She met her 'Mr. Right.' It took time for both of them to admit it, since they lived so far apart. But after several weeks they could not deny it anymore: they were in love. They spoke about it: where this could go, whether they should pursue it and what the outcome could be if they met each other. Both of them were convinced that they had to keep on talking to each other and take things day by day. Time would tell where it would lead. Time would tell whether they would still feel the way they did when the novelty wore off after several months.

Their feelings of 'being in love' deepened to love as time passed. In each other they found a soul mate. It could still go wrong when they met in real life, but neither of them worried about that. Their long distance relationship was good and solid. They rushed nothing and made no overhasty decisions. Both felt that they were meant to be together. *It was written in the stars*, they often said to each other. Soon they would hold each other for the first time, eat together, sleep together and have fun together.

Back in the bedroom, Cathy deliberately and methodically packed her suitcase. An hour later her packed suitcase stood in the corner and her room was tidy again. Cathy's eyes turned to the laptop. She checked the time on the golden watch she wore around her wrist.

"No, Cath, it's time to get to bed! The more sleep you get, the better!"

In the bathroom she took a quick shower, brushed her teeth and returned to the bedroom. She slipped under the covers naked and switched off the light. In the dark she smiled as she thought about the adventure she was embarking on. Finally, she would meet him!

Cathy's alarm sounded at three the next morning. An hour later her doorbell rang.

"I'll be there in a minute," she said to the taxi driver when she opened the door.

He took her big blue trolley suitcase with him and returned to the car to wait. One last round through her apartment assured Cathy that all lights were out and the plugs of all electrical appliances had been removed from the wall sockets. She picked up the bag she used as hand luggage and stepped outside, double-locking the front door behind her. Cathy walked to the taxi and gave the waiting driver the bag. He put it in the back with the bigger suitcase while she got into the car. Moments later he stepped in next to her, behind the steering wheel and started the fare meter.

"On to the airport," he said as he pulled away from the curb.

"Yes," Cathy smiled.

"What time are you flying?"

"Ten minutes past eight," Cathy answered.

The rest of the drive to the airport was quiet, except for the remark about traffic being light at that time of the morning, a question about the duration of Cathy's flight and another about how long before the flight she had to be at the airport.

"I prefer to be too early," Cathy told the taxi driver, "than to worry about not making it to the airport on time."

At a quarter past five Cathy paid the taxi driver. She slung the bag with her hand luggage over her shoulder along with her handbag and walked to the entrance of the airport building, pulling the blue trolley suitcase behind her. Inside the building she stopped and took a deep breath. There was something about airports that made the blood in her veins flow quicker and her heart beat faster. She smiled and walked to the information screens to see where she had to check in and at what time.

Forty-five minutes later, filled with coffee and two croissants, Cathy joined the short line at desk 11 to check in for her flight to South Africa. She handed the ground stewardess her ticket and passport and waited.

"You can put your first piece of luggage on the conveyor belt, miss," the stewardess said and smiled at Cathy.

Cathy knew her bag was well within the allowed weight for her flight. The stewardess checked the screen, printed a label for the suitcase and looped it through the handle.

"Do you have more luggage to check in?" the stewardess asked. The smile she had on her face was identical to the earlier smile. It flashed through

Cathy's mind that the fake smile made the woman's face look like a mask.

"Thank you," Cathy said as the ground stewardess pushed her passport, ticket and boarding pass towards her and wished her a good flight.

Since Cathy traveled alone, she went straight to the counter where her passport was checked again, this time by a customs officer. He glanced at her picture, then at her, closed her passport and pushed it back to her over the counter. Even though she thanked him in a friendly voice, he didn't respond.

"I guess he can't wait for his shift to end," Cathy muttered when she knew he couldn't hear her anymore.

She walked down the four steps on the other side of the customs cabin and stopped to look around her. There were lights and shops as far as she could see. The shops were another reason why she loved to be at the airport early. She rarely bought anything there, but this time it would be different. She wanted to buy something for him – something special and something she knew he couldn't get in South Africa.

With time to spare before boarding would start, Cathy walked to the gate. In her hand luggage, she now had a tiny piece of Delftware – a typical Dutch windmill – and *speculaas* cookies. She was fairly sure he wouldn't find it in the shops where he lived. Other passengers already sat in the gate waiting area. Looking for a seat, Cathy noticed a young couple who were obviously deeply in love with each other. They had their heads close together and exchanged frequent kisses. Cathy smiled and turned her head away. She found a seat next to an older couple, who held hands, their fingers entwined. Cathy wondered how long they had been together. Across from her sat a man with a grumpy expression on his face. His tousled hair and crooked tie left the impression that he had little time to get himself ready for the flight. He stared at the floor in front of him, oblivious of all the other people around him.

Just as Cathy noticed a female couple on her right, the flight attendants appeared at the counter. From experience Cathy knew that they were minutes away from being called to board. She retrieved her passport, ticket and boarding pass from her handbag and held it ready for the moment she needed to present it.

Finally, Cathy thought as she sat down in her assigned seat, 37C. She sat for about five minutes before a man asked her if he could get into his seat, which was 37A. Cathy stood up, let him pass and sat down again. She knew she would have to get up once more for the passenger who would occupy seat 37B. *Would it be a man or a woman?* Cathy wondered. It turned out to be an older woman.

"Thank you, dearie," the gray-haired lady said when she sat, grateful that Cathy got up to let her pass. Cathy smiled and nodded.

"May I ask you something?" the woman whispered, leaning closer to Cathy. Without waiting for Cathy to answer, she continued: "Please hold my hand during takeoff and landing? Those always make me so nervous!"

"I will," Cathy said and smiled. She didn't mind this request. If that was the way to make the takeoff and landing easier for this old lady, she would gladly hold her hand.

The plane filled up quick and soon they were ready to taxi towards the runway. The plane moved backwards, away from the terminal building and turned its nose into the direction of the runway. They joined the line of planes waiting to take off. The ascending planes followed each other with intervals of a few minutes. Soon Cathy heard and felt the engines of the craft gaining power as the pilot readied it for takeoff. The old lady reached for her hand and held it tight. Cathy glanced at her and saw her sitting with her head against the backrest of the seat, her eyes closed. The force of the plane moving forward pushed Cathy back into her own seat. She looked out the window and kept her eyes on the grass bordering the runway. Once the grass seemed to disappear, she knew they were airborne.

The lady next to her didn't let go of her hand. Cathy leaned towards her.
"We're in the air," she said. The only reply she got was a deep sigh from the lady. Cathy almost laughed out loud when she realized the woman had fallen asleep during takeoff. *So much for being afraid of it*, she thought with a smile. Cathy wriggled her hand free and gently laid the lady's hand in her lap. Then she did the same: she rested her head against the backrest of the seat and closed her eyes.

Her thoughts were back with the man waiting for her at the end of this long flight. The man she would finally meet in real life. At the end of this day, she would share his bed. They had looked forward to this almost from the moment they met online about a year ago. Both of them had tried hard and long to find a partner in their own countries, their own environment, their own culture, but neither of them was successful. They both reverted to the internet for friendship and maybe deep down a glimmer of hope to find a partner. That is what they had found in each other and they were convinced that their real-life-meeting would proof they were the soul mates they believed to be.

Cathy's thoughts wandered back to their last online contact. They were both thrilled because it was less than 48 hours until they would meet each other in real life. Their enthusiasm for their pending meeting soon spilled over to sexual excitement. They had played around on the webcam before, but that was more a show and tell than full-blown cybersex. However, during their last chat they went 'all the way'. It was fun and hot and exciting and only managed to build the tension for their meeting. Cathy blushed a little as she pictured herself naked in front of the webcam.

It started out silly. They played an online game of poker and then changed it into a game of strip poker. Bit by bit they took off their clothes. Even though it was now part of the strip poker game, this wasn't the first time they had seen each other naked on the webcam. There was something different this time. The sexual tension and their excitement made it different. Once they were both naked, they adjusted the rules as their game progressed.

"If you lose the next game, I want you to push a finger into your pussy. Then put it in your mouth," her online lover said.

"And if you lose it, I want you to take spit and rub it around the head of your cock," she reciprocated.

They played the next game, and she lost. In hindsight Cathy couldn't explain what had come over her. Instead of just pushing a finger into her pussy and then putting it in her mouth, she sucked her finger. She moved her finger back to her pussy, dipped inside again and repeated the sucking.

She watched him on the screen. He leaned forward, closer to the webcam, closer to his own screen. The expression on his dark face was a mixture of lust and frustration.

"Show me more," he whispered. Cathy spread her legs and put them on her desk. During the months they had gotten to know each other, she had learned to trust him enough to follow his directions.

"I want to see you masturbate," he spoke, "show me what you want me to do to you when you're here."

She smiled at him as her fingers touched her clitoris. In slow, almost exaggerated, movements she moved her index finger around her button. She pushed two fingers inside her wet hole again and spread her wetness towards the erect piece of flesh. One finger moved around in circles before a second joined it. With the fingers of her other hand she spread her labia wide.

Cathy's nipples tingled as they hardened with her growing excitement. She loved to see them stand up, erect and proud. Her eyes moved to her crotch. She had always liked to watch her fingers when she pleasured herself. This time, it was different, but still as enjoyable. Her eyes flashed back to her screen. His big eyes were fixed on her crotch. The fact that he saw what she was doing heightened her pleasure. In all earnest she fingered herself and then went back to rubbing her clitoris with those same two wet fingers. Cathy watched her hand as she repeatedly penetrated herself with her fingers and each time she tried to get deeper; each time she returned to her clitoris.

Her eyes moved back to the screen. She almost climaxed right then. He moved his big hand up and down his hard, dark brown cock. He smiled, showing his perfect white teeth. His hand didn't miss a beat. For a couple of moments their eyes locked together.

"Shall we try to come together?" he asked.

Cathy nodded. She could hold off on her orgasm for some time.

"Tell me when you're almost there," she smiled.

No more words passed through the microphones until the moment he warned her that his orgasm was close. They watched each other as they masturbated. They looked at each other's genitals, tried to learn something about the movements the other liked and smiled at each other with lust written in their eyes. Cathy climaxed only a couple of seconds after he did.

Their poker game stopped after that. They were shy afterwards, but spoke about it. That was what Cathy loved about him. He discussed things openly with her. After their cybersex experience he wanted to make sure she was okay. He told her how much he loved looking at her and that he wanted to do it again in the coming days. Cathy admitted that she longed for him; that she couldn't wait for the moment she would feel his muscular body against hers. She wanted to touch him, to trail her fingers over his beautiful dark skin. She wanted to kiss him and wanted to make him reach his orgasm while it was her hand around his cock. Their cyber orgasms did nothing to satisfy their lust for each other. In fact, it only intensified the fires of lust burning in them. Thankfully, they both expressed, in forty-eight hours they would be together.

Cathy opened her eyes. A smile lingered around her mouth. In less than eleven hours she would be there with him. She would hug him, kiss him and talk to him without a screen and ten thousand kilometers between them. Tonight she would share his bed with him. The next three weeks she would get to know him even better than she did in the past year.

"Would you like something to drink, ma'am?" the flight attendant asked, interrupting Cathy's thoughts.

"Yes, may I have a cup of tea, please?" Cathy asked and at the same time she bent down to retrieve the electronic reader from her handbag. She settled in as best as she could and started reading. Her thoughts of him were never far away, but soon the story in front of her eyes transported her to a different world, far away from the inside of the plane.

Chapter Two
Brian and Sylvia

Brian and Sylvia arrived at the airport an hour before their flight was scheduled to depart. They were just in time to check in their baggage. The ground stewardess at desk 11 smiled at the young couple as they hugged and kissed and giggled while she checked their tickets and passports. She weighed and tagged their baggage and printed their boarding passes while she wondered how long they had been a couple. Their love seemed new, like they hadn't been together for that long.

The observation of the ground stewardess was spot on. Brian and Sylvia had met each other two months before at a party of a mutual friend. They were both twenty-five, both students, but they attended different universities. Brian was the son of a government minister who had served in the previous cabinet. Sylvia was the daughter of working-class parents, who had worked hard all their lives to give Sylvia and her brother a good upbringing and education. Sylvia was serious about her studies, but since she had met Brian she had slackened. To Brian, university was a place to have fun, not to get an education. He occasionally attended class, but frequented one party after the other and paid for it with the money he made from selling drugs.

Sylvia wasn't aware that Brian dealt in drugs. She noticed that he always had enough money, but thought this was because of his rich father, who was a widower. They went to parties almost every night. Brian wanted to show her off – his beautiful and smart girlfriend. Sylvia had curves in all the right places, a symmetrical face, hazel eyes and long brown hair. When she walked into a room, men and women turned their heads. What made her even more attractive was that she was unaware of the attention she caught from people around her. She was a down-to-earth friendly girl, full of fun and laughter. Not only was she beautiful and smart, but she was a good fuck too – a combination Brian loved.

Brian understood that Sylvia would end their relationship if she found out about his drug dealing adventures. When he had just met her, he casually asked her what her opinion was on drugs. She was adamant about never trying drugs and also cutting everyone who had anything to do with it from her life. Brian wanted nothing more than to be part of her life and therefore he conveniently left out this crucial bit of information about himself. She never asked him where he got his money. To make sure she suspected nothing, he sometimes allowed her to pay for drinks, but mainly he was the one doing the paying.

A month into their relationship, he told Sylvia that he wanted to take her to the island of Mauritius. Sylvia protested, but Brian pushed. He promised to pay for everything; that Sylvia didn't have to worry about the money-side of their trip. Sylvia mentioned her studies, and that she was running behind as it was. She could not just take time off from it during the semester. For every point she brought up in protest, Brian stated two reasons why she should join him for the trip. Eventually Sylvia caved. There was nothing else she could think of. All of Brian's reasons for her to join him sounded perfect. For three weeks she worked hard to get up to date again with her course work and even worked ahead. Then, a week before their flight would leave, the partying started. What Brian hadn't told Sylvia about the trip was the primary purpose of the flight. He had to pick up drugs to bring back home. If he wanted to keep up the same lifestyle he had in the past few years, he needed more drugs to sell.

Brian took their passports and papers from the ground stewardess and stuffed it in the side pocket of the carry-on bag he had with him. He thanked the stewardess, planted a kiss on Sylvia's mouth and pulled her towards the customs counter with him. The customs officer was unimpressed with the loving couple in front of him.

"One at a time, please!" he barked when both of them stood in front of his counter.

Brian quickly stepped back behind the yellow line after he had given Sylvia her passport, ticket and boarding pass. She pouted when she handed it to the grumpy officer. Getting through customs was quick and soon the lovebirds were together again. Brian put his arm around Sylvia's shoulder and she leaned against him, lifting her face to him for another kiss.

"I want you," she whispered.

Brian's cock stirred in his pants. It had been three hours since the last time they had made love, but just like her he was ready again. He wanted to feel her pussy around his cock, feel how she squeezed his hard member with her tight muscles to milk his cum from him.

"Where?" he asked.

"The restrooms?" she suggested.

They looked around. Despite the early hour the tax-free shopping area was crowded with people. This international airport was busy at all times of day, except for the early hours of the morning.

"Let's go to the gate," Brian suggested, "there'll be restrooms over there too and maybe less people than here."

Hand in hand they followed the signs that showed the way towards their gate. Brian was right. The farther they moved from the main shopping area, the quieter it became. There were still people around when they approached their gate, but it was less crowded. They passed the gate and walked to the restrooms on the other side of it. Each of them dashed into the respective restrooms for their gender to check how busy it was inside. Brian already waited for Sylvia when she returned from the ladies' room. She looked around, saw that no one paid them any attention and grabbed Brian's hand. Sylvia pulled him into the ladies' room with her. He wanted to protest, but she swiftly opened the broom closet inside the ladies' room and pulled him with her.

The broom closet was barely big enough for Brian to fit with his wide frame. A faint light overhead gave just enough light to see each other. Sylvia pulled Brian closer and kissed him. Her hands were on his crotch, fondling his half hard cock through the fabric of his pants. Brian's hands found her breasts. He squeezed and weighed and kneaded the flesh. Sylvia moaned and broke off the kiss. She fumbled with his belt and then the button of his pants. Once undone, she pushed his pants and boxer shorts to his knees in the same movement as her crouching down. His hard cock sprang free from its confinements and bounced up and down in front of Sylvia's eyes. She giggled and caught it in her mouth, holding onto Brian's legs. He looked down at her and smiled. She was such a naughty, vibrant girl. Never did a woman make him feel so good. Every day he fell in love with her a little bit more. He had never experienced one dull moment with Sylvia in the short time they had been together.

Sylvia steadied herself with one hand against the wall of the broom closet and the other around Brian's penis. She licked around the head of his cock, teasing him with her tongue. Her eyes were on his face, watching as he tried to keep his grunting to a minimum. In one quick movement, she took all of his cock into her mouth. The tip of his member pressed against the back of her throat. She held it there as long as she could keep down her gag reflex. Spit dripped from her mouth onto her chin and the floor. She went back to licking only the tip of the blood-filled flesh. Sylvia took him deep into her mouth a second time, and when she withdrew again, Brian grabbed her shoulders and pulled her up towards him. She thought he wanted to kiss her, but Brian swung her around, pushed her forward, pulled her dress up and yanked her panties to the side.

He buried himself deep inside her, pulled out and slammed back into her, not worried about hurting her. Sylvia pushed herself up onto her tiptoes to give him easy access. Brian fucked her deep and hard. He took possession of her body as he had done so many times in the past. He still caused butterflies to flutter around in her stomach and this time was no different. She tingled all over. Excitement filled her body from the crown of her hair to the tips of her toes. Brian slammed into her one last time and with a low grunt coming from deep in his throat, he climaxed inside her. Sylvia had no orgasm, but she didn't mind. Feeling Brian inside her, experiencing his intense lust, was enough for her.

She turned around to face him. He pulled her closer. Their tongues touched as they gently kissed. Brian's hand moved down to Sylvia's crotch, but at that moment they heard voices on the other side of the door. Both froze. They stood still for several seconds, not knowing whether they heard other passengers or the cleaning staff. If it was the cleaning staff, they would be discovered any moment. Quickly they straightened their clothes. They waited several minutes longer until everything seemed silent on the other side of the door. Brian pushed the door open a crack. He glanced back at Sylvia and put his finger on his lips, hushing her. Through the crack in the door he watched the woman at the mirror. She checked her make-up and hair and only when it was to her satisfaction, she grabbed her bag and walked towards Brian. He thought she looked right at him, but she disappeared from sight. Nothing happened.

Brian reached back for Sylvia's hand, pushed open the broom closet door and pulled his girlfriend with him. Just as they rounded the corner to leave the ladies' room, two women entered from the hallway. They dashed passed them. Sylvia burst out in laughter when they reached the hallway and together they walked back towards the gate.

"That was only the start of a wonderful holiday," Brian said as he stopped to pull her closer. They kissed and didn't care about standing in the way of other people wanting to get to their gates.

"Will you join the club with me?" Brian whispered in Sylvia's ear.

"Which club?" she asked him with confusion written all over her face.

"Ever heard of the mile-high club?"

"Oh yes," Sylvia giggled, "I would love to join."

With their hands locked together and smiles on their faces, they continued to the gate, where they joined the other waiting passengers.

Brian and Sylvia found their seats at the back of the plane. Brian was in seat 67H and Sylvia in seat 67K. They had the privilege of having no one sitting with them as this part of the row had only two seats.

The loving couple immediately saw the possibility increasing to join the so-called mile-high club. They were three hours into the flight when the opportunity arose to reach their goal. Up to then they had kept busy with reading, kissing, listening to music, more kissing and having something to drink and snack. They studied the movements of the flight attendants and realized that when drinks were served, the attendants worked in sections from the front to the back. During that time no personnel was in the back of the aircraft. Just as the flight attendants started to serve another round of drinks, Brian and Sylvia reclined their seats. They took the thin airline blankets, covered themselves and pretended to lie down together to sleep. The armrest between their seats was in the upright position.

Brian had his back turned to the aisle, lying on his right side. His left arm was draped over Sylvia's hips. Sylvia lay on her right side too and Brian spooned with her. To the innocent onlooker, it was as if the couple was asleep. Brian's arm concealed the movement under the blanket. His right arm was between them, guiding his cock between Sylvia's pussy lips. Sylvia had her dress pulled up and her panties to the side. Her pussy was still slick with the semen Brian had pumped into her when he fucked her in the broom closet. Brian slipped into her with ease. He moved as little as possible, not wanting to draw any attention to them.

"You'll have to do the work, my love. Careful, not too much moving," he whispered in her ear.

Sylvia knew what he meant. She moved her hips a fraction, causing Brian to slip deeper into her. Then, with minimal movement, but a lot of clenching and releasing of her pussy muscles, she massaged his hardness. Brian buried his face in her long, brown hair and pressed his lips tightly on each other. He knew he should not make any sound, or people would catch on to what they were doing. With the ever-present sexual tension between them, it didn't take Sylvia long to draw Brian's orgasm from him. This time she wanted an orgasm too. Brian sensed it. They turned around and Sylvia snuggled up to his back. His right hand was still under the blanket, but behind him and between Sylvia's legs. He concentrated on rubbing her clitoris, pressing down hard to bring her to a quick climax. The cart with drinks was halfway down the aisle towards them. Time was running out. Sylvia lifted her right leg to make more room and tensed her buttock muscles, pushing her cunt against Brian's hand. A tiny squeak escaped her mouth as she climaxed. A woman on the other side of the aisle glanced at them, but she returned to her book, satisfied that the couple seemed to be asleep.

Soon after their coupling, they both drifted off to sleep and only woke when the flight attendants served lunch two hours later. By then the sexual tension between them started building again.

Chapter Three
Anthony

Anthony rushed out the door of the airport hotel and followed the signs to departures, where he had to check in for his flight back home. He flew in from London the night before and spent the night in the airport hotel. In fact, he could have flown home directly from London, but there was no way to explain that to his wife. She thought that he had been in Amsterdam for the last two weeks, running a business course. The truth was that the course had lasted only five days, and the rest of the time he spent in London with Cassidy.

For the past six months, Cassidy had not only been his secretary, but also his lover. She was young and beautiful, full of life and fun and she loved sex. Anthony couldn't remember the last time he had sex with his wife. Not even his upcoming trip could move her to any kind of intimacy with him, even though it would take him away from home for two weeks. Despite being in an almost sexless marriage, Anthony didn't want to leave his wife. Some of his mates stayed in their unhappy marriages because of their children, but Anthony did not do it for the same reason. No, Anthony stayed with his wife because when he forgot about the lack of sex, they were the perfect couple. He still loved her as much as he loved her from the moment they had met, despite her lack of desire.

Anthony had a healthy appetite for sex. If his wife didn't want to give him what he needed, he had to look for it outside the marriage. That was his reasoning and the way he soothed his conscience every time he fucked Cassidy. If his wife should ever find out about his affair, their marriage would end. She would never tolerate his infidelity. Anthony caught a glimpse of himself in the mirror as he rode the lift to the next floor. He was an attractive man. All his adult life he had taken good care of his body, trying to compensate for the facial scars left by teenage acne. He wore a dark gray suit, off-white shirt and a tie with off-white, dark gray and blue stripes. His dark brown hair had streaks of silver, giving him a sophisticated look. Anthony knew that if it weren't for his looks and the position he had in the company, Cassidy wouldn't have shown any interest in him. He was more than double her age. Another thing Anthony suspected was that their affair would be over as soon as there was someone higher up the corporate ladder Cassidy could fuck.

Anthony found the desk where he had to be. He joined the check-in line and as they shuffled forward in a slow, but steady pace, his thoughts wandered off again.

Cassidy caught Anthony's attention because of her appearance. She was one of five women who applied for the job as his secretary. Even though she had not been the candidate with the best papers, she got the job. Cassidy looked like a model. With her slender body she could easily have made it to the catwalk. The high-heeled shoes she always wore accentuated her long legs. Her straight, shiny blond hair just touched the upper rounding of her buttocks. Sometimes she wore it to the front, where it covered her full, round breasts. Every day it seemed like she went to the beauty parlor before she came to the office. Her eye make-up was perfectly done and her full lips always showed a soft shade of pink lipstick. Cassidy carried herself in a way evident from what she had learned at the finishing school in France. To top off her striking appearance, her melodious voice was pleasant to listen to.

Once she started working for Anthony, he learned more about her. Her father recently lost most of their money on the stock exchange. They had to sell their house in the suburbs and moved to an apartment in the city. All friends of her parents disappeared when they were out of money and not able to entertain the same way they did before. Cassidy was a fighter and determined to make a success of her career as an executive secretary, even if it meant fucking her way to the top.

The unexpected opportunity for Anthony to run the business course abroad, presented itself when a colleague fell ill. The managing director appointed Anthony to take his colleague's place as trainer. Anthony had only one week to prepare for the trip and to work out his notes for the course. Cassidy worked long days to help him with the preparations. Without her he wouldn't have been able to do it. During the evenings they worked together, a plan formed in Anthony's mind. He gave his secretary time off, but what no one else knew was that he also gave her a ticket to fly to London, including a hotel reservation. She would leave two days after Anthony's departure to Amsterdam. Anthony told his wife he had to be in Amsterdam a couple of days before the course started and that, after the course, he would stay several days longer to wrap up things. However, after only five days in Amsterdam, on the evening of the day that the course ended, Anthony flew to London. Together with Cassidy he checked into a four-star hotel just on the other side of Westminster Bridge from the Big Ben. Their room had a spectacular view over Thames and the monumental parliament building.

Cassidy's hotel was on the other side of the Thames, close to the Victoria Embankment. Her room was paid for one more week, but she moved in with Anthony for the rest of the eight days they would be in London. In the same way, Anthony still had his hotel room in the center of Amsterdam. Anthony arrived in London just after noon. Cassidy already waited for him in the lobby of their hotel. The moment the door of their room closed behind them, they were all over each other. Anthony trapped Cassidy between his body and the door, kissing her hard and passionate while his hands grabbed her skirt and pulled at it. His erection hurt with longing when he found her naked sex. She wore no panties under her skirt, only a garter belt and stockings. His fingers entered her waiting sex.

Cassidy fumbled with his belt and pants and finally succeeded in pushing his pants down and then his underpants. Her hand closed around his hard cock and she swung her right leg up around his hips. Anthony understood what she wanted. He wanted the same. With urgency in their movements, as if there was no time left to be together, she guided him inside her. He grabbed her buttocks and lifted her onto him. Cassidy swung her other leg around him too and put her arms around his neck. Anthony's knees were bent as he pushed into Cassidy, bobbing her up and down on his cock. Cassidy squealed as he slammed into her repeatedly. The pain of her leg and arm muscles screaming for release mixed with the pleasure of his thick cock filling her wet pussy. Anthony abruptly stopped moving when he climaxed deep inside Cassidy.

Their position made it almost impossible for Cassidy to climax. Anthony awkwardly carried her to the bed, her arms and legs still around him and his pants around his ankles. He dropped her on the bed on her back. Her hand disappeared between her legs. Anthony loved to watch her touch herself and Cassidy loved to give a show. Anthony kicked his pants off and pulled the desk chair closer to the bed. He sat back to enjoy the performance. Cassidy had two fingers in her cunt, moving them in and out. His semen covered her fingers, which she soon spread to her erect clitoris. She loved to tease herself by softly touching her flesh, sending a tingly sensation through her loins, but Cassidy didn't like climaxing by clitoral stimulation only. She preferred penetration, whether by fingers, cock or a toy.

Cassidy spread her legs wide, tightening the muscles in her upper legs. She pushed three fingers into her pussy and fucked herself at a steady pace. Her fingers moved back to her clitoris and teased the bundle of nerve endings for seconds before she finger-fucked herself again. Over and over she did this and as Anthony watched, he caught onto the rhythm of her movements. Her breathing got heavier; her moaning louder. Her free hand moved to her breasts, kneading and crushing them, hurting them. She increased the pace at which she fingered herself and rubbed her clitoris. In. Out. In out. In out. Rub-rub-rub. In. Out. In. Out. Anthony almost lost track of her movements. He loved when she showed off like this. She knew her body well and was confident in sharing this intimacy with him. In-out-rub-rub. In-out-rub-rub. In-out-in-out-in. Cassidy drew her breath in and her back arched. Her orgasm squirted from her body as she climaxed. Fluids landed on the bed and on the floor. Cassidy cupped her pussy with both hands, trying to still the throbbing. Anthony lay down next to her. His cock was ready for the next round.

They fucked on and off all afternoon – on the bed, on the couch, on the desk, in front of the window that faced the Big Ben and under the shower before they got dressed to go out for dinner. Dinner followed in a restaurant on the South Bank, facing the river Thames. Anthony told Cassidy about the business course he ran in the Netherlands; about things they could improve for the next time. They talked about the differences and similarities in the culture of their home country and the countries in Europe. Many subjects came up between them, but the one thing they didn't discuss was their relationship. Neither wanted to make the other promises they couldn't keep. Anthony and Cassidy enjoyed their affair, but neither wanted a future with the other. They only used each other for their own selfish reasons.

They filled their days in London with a variety of excursions like every other tourist in London did, such as shopping in Oxford Street, but also at Piccadilly Circus and in Harrods. At Buckingham Palace they witnessed the Changing of the Guard and then went for a walk through Hyde Park. On one day they visited the Westminster Abbey and St. Paul's Cathedral and on the other they went for two rides in the London Eye. They spent another day in Greenwich and they visited Abbey Road, after which The Beatles named their last studio LP. Sometimes they stayed out all day. Other days they returned to the hotel for an hour or two, where they fucked until they went out again.

It was on one of those afternoons, right after they had toured London by city tourist bus, that Anthony had a new and exciting sexual experience. It started out the same as many other days. Their feet hurt after hours of walking. Both kicked their shoes off and lay down on bed, on top of the covers. No matter how tired they were, something always seemed to draw them together. Soon they kissed, fondled and undressed. Anthony's hands were on Cassidy's breasts, grabbing and squeezing the flesh between his fingers until she moaned. Cassidy closed her hand around Anthony's cock, satisfied that he was hard and ready to fuck her. He moved his mouth to Cassidy's nipple and his fingers found her wet entrance. Anthony bit lightly on and around her nipple, while he finger-fucked her to her first orgasm.

Cassidy surprised Anthony by pushing him back on the bed and kneeling between his legs. He watched as she took his erection in her mouth. First only the tip disappeared between her lipstick-pink lips. Her tongue swirled around the head. Cassidy opened her mouth wide and allowed saliva to drip down her lover's cock. Her eyes never left his face. She licked up and down his length and, each time she reached the top, she took the tip of his cock in her mouth. Anthony had to work hard at holding back on his climax. He almost shot his load up in the air when she licked his balls and her tongue just barely touched his asshole. Afraid he might climax too soon and filled with an urge to fuck her hard, Anthony switched places with Cassidy. He was in her within seconds. He rammed his cock into her waiting cunt and, wanting to reach deeper, he hooked her legs over his upper arms. Cassidy's ass lifted off the bed and her cunt spread wide open.

Anthony pulled his cock out almost entirely and pushed back in hard. His pace was quick and his need to climax high. At one point, he pulled out too far but didn't notice. His cock slipped down a fraction and when he wanted to push in again, he met some resistance. He looked down and saw he was pushing against Cassidy's anus. Anthony held still, looked at Cassidy who nodded, and then he pushed harder.

His cock needed guidance, and a bit of lubrication. Anthony sat back on his legs, with his cock still against Cassidy's darker opening. He held it in his hand, spit down on it and then he pushed. Cassidy bent her legs and reached down with her hands to pull her buttocks apart. She offered him her dark hole. Bit by bit Anthony pushed into her ass. It surprised him how tight and warm it was and he watched in amazement as his cock slipped inside her with relative ease. Cassidy drew her breath in, partly from pain, but mostly from excitement. Her cunt glistened with a slick wetness that dripped down to her ass, helping to lubricate her asshole for the intrusion. Anthony pushed in up to his balls.

"Fuck me," Cassidy pleaded, "please, fuck my ass."

Anthony didn't need more encouragement than that. He pulled out until just the tip was still inside her. He spat on his cock again and pushed back in. Each time he pushed back in, he met less resistance. His pace quickened as his own passion took over. He fucked her ass in the same pace he did her pussy. Cassidy's fingers slipped into her wet cunt. She felt him moving against her fingers through the thin wall that separated the two holes from each other. Her cunt was dripping wet, reflecting the intense lust she felt. She moved her fingers to her clitoris. Once again, Anthony was amazed by how well this young woman knew her own body. *If only my wife...* He pushed the thought away and increased his fucking speed. Cassidy accepted the pounding and rubbed her clitoris harder. Anthony climaxed first. His body stiffened and his cock contracted as he spurted his semen in Cassidy's dark hole. The contractions of Anthony's cock inside her were just the bit of extra stimulation Cassidy needed to reach her own climax.

Anthony collapsed next to Cassidy and tried to catch his breath.

"Thank you," Cassidy said.

"It was a first for me," Anthony admitted and Cassidy only smiled. She was not prepared to share information about her earlier lovers, or admit to him how much she loved anal sex. Anthony fucked her ass more times while they were in London. Cassidy didn't mind his new fixation.

Cassidy was insatiable and towards the end of their eight-day stay, Anthony tried to stay out for as long as possible during their day trips. He longed to be back home; to quiet evenings with his wife. They would be sexless evenings, but loving, happy and relaxed ones. He wanted to get back to how things were; to where he enjoyed his wife's company and occasionally fucked Cassidy. The last day they were in London, Cassidy proposed to stay in the hotel room, but Anthony opted for some last-minute shopping. There was a bit of a strain between them as they walked between the shops on Piccadilly Circus. Cassidy's mood finally improved when they returned to their room late in the afternoon and Anthony fucked her. He had already packed his bags and after an early dinner in one of the hotel's restaurants, Anthony and Cassidy checked out. Anthony had to catch the last flight out to Amsterdam. They kissed and Anthony waved at Cassidy through the back window of the taxi as they sped off to London City Airport. Cassidy returned to her hotel on Victoria Embankment. She would fly back to South Africa later the next day.

On his return in Amsterdam, Anthony checked into the airport hotel, put his stuff in his room and called the front desk for a taxi. His trip took him back to the hotel he was in before he went to London.

"Please wait here. I'll be back in a minute," Anthony said to the taxi driver and got out of the car.

He dropped the envelope with his checkout papers and key cards in the night box of the hotel, where they would find it the next morning. Anthony returned to the airport hotel with the same taxi and was thankful to be alone at last. No matter how much he had enjoyed his naughty adventures with Cassidy, Anthony was happy that he could at least get one night of unbroken sleep.

He woke from his daydreaming when one of his fellow passengers tapped his shoulder. He turned around and saw a busty, platinum blond woman smiling at him. A huge pair of sunglasses hid her eyes from the world. He looked at her, confused.

"You're next," she said as she pointed to the desks.

"Oh... err... uhh... thank you," he stuttered and his face turned red with embarrassment. He was so caught up in re-living the sexy times with Cassidy that he had come to the front of the line without being aware of it. Anthony grabbed his carry-on bag and proceeded to the counter. A ground stewardess greeted him with a fake smile, irritation showing in her eyes. Anthony didn't notice.

In the gate waiting area he busied himself with his phone. He sent his wife a text message: *I'm ready to board the plane. Can't wait to see you tonight!*

He had been in touch with her at irregular times while he was in London. His wife had confronted him with that in a text message. His excuse was that the course was crazily busy and chaotic. Anthony followed his first text with another: *Can't wait to get out of this chaotic place and be in our quiet home, where you organized everything so perfectly.*

He figured that he needed to sweet-talk her, since he had neglected her in the past couple of days.

Anthony sent his last text to his wife just after he had buckled himself into his seat: *I'm in the plane. See you tonight, darling. I love you!*

Chapter Four
Harriet and Angie

Angie smiled at Harriet as they buckled into their seats. They were excited to make this trip. Few students had the time or the opportunity to go backpacking for three months during the summer holidays, let alone doing that abroad. Their parents received the news about their traveling plans with a huge amount of enthusiasm. Getting their children to go out in the big wide world to explore had always been a priority with the parents. Since the young women would go backpacking in a group of about twenty students coming from all over the world, their parents were reassured that they would be safe during their time in South Africa.

"Are you as excited as I am," Harriet asked her friend.

"Oh yes, I am," Angie said.

She hoped her friend couldn't tell that it was a partial lie. For Angie this was not only a nice adventure, but also an escape. Two days before they were to leave for their trip, Angie had discovered that she was pregnant.

Ten weeks ago Angie and Harriet went out with a group of friends. There was one male student in the group that Angie had fancied for months, but he never noticed her, until that evening in the bar. Even though Angie really wanted his attention, she was suddenly nervous when she realized that he was as interested in her as she was in him. Or, so she thought. It was only later that the evening that they chatted. He bought her a drink and flirted with her. Harriet interrupted them.

"Are you okay if I leave earlier? I have to study for a test," Harriet asked.

"Of course. Go. I will be okay," Angie answered.

"I will bring Angie home," the young man jumped in.

It was not uncommon for Harriet or Angie to leave the other at one of their hangouts when either one of them had to study. Hitching rides from other students was more a rule than an exception. Everyone did it.

Angie and the male student sat close together at the corner of the bar. They talked about their studies and their dreams for the future. He surprised Angie when he kissed her without warning, but she didn't mind. She kissed him back, finally able to show her interest and attraction to him.

"Shall we have one more drink and then leave?" he asked and Angie nodded. She was somewhat light-headed after the drinks she already had, but she thought she could handle another one. Angie didn't want to come across as a party-pooper by refusing the last drink. Half an hour later, the male student unlocked the door on the passenger's side for Angie to get into his car. He walked around and got in behind the steering wheel. Angie gave him her street address and he started the car. He turned the nose of the car into the wrong direction.

"You had to go left, not right," she said.

"I know," he said, "but I first want to show you something."

His kind smile put her at ease. She relaxed and soon recognized that he was driving towards a nearby seaside town.

He parked the car in a darker spot of the parking area and turned to Angie. She smiled at him and blushed. He pulled her closer and they kissed. His hand moved to her breast and when Angie started to pull away, he made soothing sounds and didn't take his lips off hers. In her confusion, Angie didn't know whether to push him away or continue kissing him. She opted for the last, reasoning that him fondling her breasts was not the end of the world. Minutes later he pulled away, reached over her and reclined her seat. He moved over to sit on the same seat with her. It was a tight fit. They kissed again and his hand moved back to her breasts, but this time under her top. Again Angie made feeble attempts to pull away and again he made soothing sounds, which made her feel ridiculous.

It was when his hand moved down to the hem of her skirt that she stopped him.

"No, please, I don't want this," she said.

"Are you sure?" he asked in a tone that made her feel like a fool. Angie didn't answer him right away and apparently he saw that as permission to continue. When he did, she pushed his hand away, but he ignored it. His fingers touched her crotch.

"Oh, I believe you are wet," he chuckled.

Angie wanted to die. She stayed still, almost not breathing. Her mind was working overtime, but her body was passive.

Why didn't I go home with Harriet? Why am I such a coward? I should demand that he takes me home, dammit! How am I going to stop him? What if he hurts me? Or worse?

She blushed when the next thought popped into her mind.

Why am I wet?

Harriet was the more outspoken one of the two students. Angie was the soft and sentimental one and frequently didn't dare to stand up for herself. She found herself in a situation she didn't know how to handle. She was still contemplating what to do when the male student pushed her seat back as far as it could go. He rolled over on top of her. Angie fought him, but he was too strong.

"No please, no," she said as he held her arms down with ease.

"Come on girl," he said, "it's clear you want this as much as I do. Your cunt is so fucking wet, so stop pretending to be a prude."

Afterwards Angie couldn't recall the exact details. She remembered that he positioned himself between her legs, pulled her panties aside and pushed his hard cock into her. She didn't know when he took it out of his pants. Angie fought him. She fought him hard. She said 'no' over and over again. Angie had tried to push him off her, but he grabbed her wrists and pinned them above her head.

"Ah, you like it rough, don't you?" he said as he fucked her.

Angie wriggled and tried to free herself but then he pinned her down with his forearm across her chest, pressing the air from her lungs.

"Stay still, bitch, or..." he growled as he continued pushing into her. Afraid to move, she just lay there, allowing him to fuck her. Tears burned in the corners of her eyes. She turned her head away so he couldn't see them. The few minutes until he blew his load inside her, lasted a lifetime. She was home half an hour later and went straight to bathroom. Angie showered and scrubbed herself between her legs until she was raw and hurting. Tears streamed down her face, mixing in with the water of the shower. The sound of the falling water muffled her sobs. Thankfully, her parents were asleep already. She couldn't bear facing them in this state.

Angie didn't sleep that night. She cried and just when she was about to fall asleep, she started sobbing again. She always thought he was so kind, a gentleman, but he turned out to be a monster. He fucked her even though she told him she didn't want it; even though she fought him and tried to push him off her. He raped her. No one will ever believe her.

Why didn't I fight harder? I should have stopped him. Why did I allow him to touch my breasts? It was all my fault. I should have stopped him when he put his hand under my skirt. I didn't fight him hard enough. Why was I wet? No one will ever believe me.

Angie had dark rings under her eyes when she got up the next morning. She chastised herself throughout the night and didn't stop when she finally got out of bed. Angie's parents had gone to work. She was alone in the house. Angie couldn't bring herself to go to class. When she tried to eat something, the food didn't stay down for long. She went back to bed, still sobbing. Angie drifted into a restless sleep early in the afternoon, exhausted.

The next day Angie felt better. Physically better, but not mentally. Angie's thoughts kept on returning to that night. She had to tell someone, but the thought that no one might believe her, made her keep her mouth shut. She was angry with herself that she hadn't stopped him and she was angry with herself that she was too afraid to report him. Not afraid of the police, but afraid of not being believed. She wished for once she could stop over-thinking things and just do what was right. Days went by and Angie was in a constant battle with herself. Over and over she deliberated whether she should go to the police or not. Then she took the easy way out: two weeks after the rape she decided that too much time had passed. She should have gone to the police right after the rape. It was too late now and it was time to concentrate on the future.

Angie poured herself into her studies. She studied until late at night, until she could barely keep her eyes open anymore. Then, she fell into a deep, dreamless sleep and woke up early the next morning to study before she went to class. It was almost the end of the study year and she would have a series of tests soon. She wanted to be prepared for it. This was not the only reason for studying so hard. She allowed her studies to occupy her thoughts, because it pushed the memories of the rape to the back of her mind. Angie declined invitations from Harriet to go out for drinks. Each time she used studying as an excuse and Harriet didn't mind. To study for tests was always more important than going out with friends. The two students saw each other between classes and it was like old times, although Angie was stressed and absentminded at times. Harriet noticed it, but she thought that Angie worried about the upcoming tests.

Four weeks after the rape, Harriet and Angie saw an advert on the notice board of their faculty for a backpacking tour to South Africa. They really wanted to make the trip, but they needed to discuss it with their parents. It would take them away from home for three months and even though they had savings, they needed their parents to finance part of the trip. They were delirious with joy when their parents agreed. The planning of what to pack for the trip started. They studied the itinerary the international tourist agency had sent them. They also received a list of names of the other backpackers and their countries of residence. Harriet and Angie were as excited as two kids on Christmas Eve, but they first had to get the tests of the last two weeks of the semester out of the way.

Eight weeks after the rape, Angie got sick. Each afternoon, about an hour after she had her lunch, she was nauseous and sometimes she had to vomit. She didn't relate it to her lunch, but thought she was tired after studying late hours every evening for weeks, and all the excitement around their upcoming trip. She was sure the nausea would disappear once they started their summer adventure.

In the weeks since they were together in the bar and Harriet had left Angie with the attractive male student, Harriet hadn't only been studying. She studied a lot, but Harriet also had an affair with one of her lecturers. It started months earlier, when she needed help on a specific part of the textbook and stayed in the class after the rest had left. She asked the lecturer to explain it again. It was only that afternoon she realized how charming he was, and that he was only four years older than her. He took his time to explain the part she didn't understand and even did it a second and third time. He only stopped when she could repeat everything he had explained to her. Then he invited her for a drink.

Lecturers and students were forbidden to have relationships, but they were allowed to discuss course work in a public establishment. Under the guise of 'extra lessons' they left the books visible on the table while they had a drink together and talked about themselves. They went out to the same place many times, evening after evening, before he invited Harriet to his place. He gave her the address and left her in the coffee shop where they had met. Harriet had another cup of coffee. An hour later, he buzzed open the street door to his apartment building and Harriet rode the lift to his floor. The moment his front door closed behind her, he pulled her into his embrace and kissed her hard. Harriet's hands moved to the buttons on his shirt and she undid it. He pulled her T-shirt from her denims and slipped it over her head, trapping her arms inside the T-shirt above her head.

His body pressed against hers as he kissed her again. They almost tore the clothes from each other's bodies. By the time they reached his bedroom, the apartment looked like something from a movie. Clothes and shoes formed a trail from the front door to the bedroom. He quickly turned her around and pinned her arms behind her back, holding onto her wrists with one hand. With the other, he pushed her forward onto the bed. Harriet heard him open a drawer and then the tear of a condom wrapper. He entered her from behind. She lifted herself on her tiptoes to allow him to enter her deep.

"Yes, yes, yes," she moaned, "oh yes, fuck me hard."

He complied, ramming his cock in and out. Harriet moaned and talked and climaxed and talked more. He fucked her as hard as he could manage until his body suddenly stiffened and he climaxed too.

They lay together on the bed afterwards, talking and laughing and relaxing. Harriet threw her leg over and straddled him.

"What are you doing?" he asked.

"Wait and see," she said as she bent forward and kissed him on the lips. Then she kissed his neck, his chest, his nipples and down his stomach until she reached the fuzz of pubic hair. His cock was half hard. By then he understood what she was about to do. He had his hands behind his head and watched as Harriet closed her lips around the head of his cock. Her tongue flicked around the tip, teasing him. There was fun and lust in her eyes. She watched him when she slowly lowered her mouth to take in more of his cock. The more of his hard member she took in her mouth, the broader he smiled. Her lips touched his pubic hair. She held the position for a moment and only moved her mouth back up when she almost gagged.

Over and over she took him in deep before she fucked him with her mouth. She closed her hand around the base of his cock and it followed the movements of her hand. She sucked him hard, licked him softly and teased him by flicking her tongue over his frenulum. By now he had closed his eyes. His breathing was heavy.

"Can I... uh... will you... uh... is it okay... uh..." he stuttered.

"I will swallow, if that's what you mean," Harriet blurted and then continued to suck him.

That was what he wanted to know. He didn't hold back anymore. Only minutes later he climaxed for a second time that evening, spurting his cum into her waiting mouth. Harriet swallowed every drop and licked him clean, enjoying how his cock went softer against her tongue.

He used two more condoms that night before Harriet went home in the small hours of the morning. Their relationship bloomed. Not only did they have wonderful sex, but they talked about almost every subject under the sun, still pretending he was giving her extra lessons. Harriet wanted to tell the world she was in love – *or was it lust?* – but she didn't want to get him into trouble. It was always the lecturers who lost their jobs when the management heard about an affair. Harriet kept it a secret. She hoped their relationship would last forever. After her graduation, she would scream it from the rooftops that they were a couple.

In the last two weeks before their trip Harriet and Angie saw little of each other. They were following different courses and had tests at different times. When they could, they got together to discuss their trip. They were both excited, but at times Angie was more subdued than Harriet knew her. Harriet took that as a sign that Angie was her worrying self – worrying about the trip and worrying about her tests.

"Everything will be okay," Harriet said and hugged her friend.

Angie almost told Harriet what bothered her. She still had nauseous spells and something had dawned on her. She wanted to do a test, but she was afraid to do so. What would Harriet think of her if she knew how stupid she had been? She wouldn't be able to bear the contempt of her friend.

Angie wrote her last test three days before their departure to South Africa and Harriet wrote her last one a day later, in the morning. The two friends had an appointment to go shopping for the last necessities in the afternoon. That morning Angie went to the drug store. She bought a pregnancy test and cycled back home. Her parents were at work. Angie knew the answer before she saw it on the test. The rape of ten weeks before had left her pregnant. She sagged to the floor on the bathroom.

What should I do? Keep it? Abort it? How can I ever tell mom and dad I'm pregnant?

Even if she had a boyfriend it would have been terrible to disappoint them like this. They had such great plans for her and yes, children were part of that plan, but not just yet. Then a thought struck her – she would find an opportunity to have an abortion done in South Africa. Her mind hooked on that idea. That was her way out. It would always be her secret – the rape, the pregnancy and the abortion.

The two students were at the airport far too early on the day they departed on their big adventure. Their parents wanted them all to have coffee together before their daughters went through customs. When at last Harriet and Angie went through customs, they giggled like two teenagers. At last, *at last* the day they had been looking forward to for weeks was here. They were on their way to the gate where their plane would leave. Their big adventure was about to start. They were elated, but both carried a secret and it was present constantly in the back of their minds. Harriet wanted to tell Angie about her lover and Angie wanted to confide in her friend. Neither of them told the other, each for their own reasons.

In the waiting area they sat on the tip of their chairs, waiting impatiently to be called to board the plane. When the business class passengers moved forward, they stood up, only to sit down again, both blushing. Then, finally, economic class passengers could board. Angie and Harriet quickly joined the line and had their passports and boarding tickets checked by a friendly flight attendant. They found their seats in the plane and as they buckled into their seats, Angie smiled at Harriet. Excitement and fear made her shiver. Excitement for their trip and fear for the plan she wanted to execute in South Africa. Next to her, Harriet looked through the porthole window. *I will be back soon*, she said in her mind, thinking about her lover.

Chapter Five
Edward and Nora

"Hands in your lap," Edward said without looking at Nora, who sat in the seat next to him. They were in seats 67A and 67B, with Edward in the aisle seat.

"Yes, Sir," Nora said and lay her hands next to each other in her lap, her palms turned upwards.

"Good girl," Edward smiled at her. Nora smiled back at him, content not to move until he instructed her otherwise.

Edward and Nora had been a couple for close to twenty years. They got married eighteen years ago and for the last ten years of their marriage, they had been in a BDSM relationship. They were thankful to be part of a small percentage of couples who managed to have a successful kink relationship inside their marriage. Edward was the dominant partner and Nora was the submissive. They didn't just wake up one morning and decided that they were dominant and submissive. No, it was part of their personalities for as long as they could remember. Through the first ten years of being together there were elements of dominance and submission in their relationship. Neither Edward nor Nora recognized it as BDSM elements, simply because it was so much a part of who they were. Their sex included rough play and pain, but no rules. Both of them came to a point where they wanted to take it to a higher level and give it more structure. That was when they committed themselves to actively explore a relationship in which they would have unequal roles.

Even though elements of BDSM were always present in their relationship, they had a lot to learn to make a success of this new facet of their lives. They needed time to find a new balance. The couple agreed on a set of rules for Nora. Where in the past she always ran things by Edward before deciding what to do, she now had the instruction to do so. It was just a change of her mindset, not of the actual way she handled things. Nora liked this. She liked to feel Edward's control over her. She needed it. Nora was in control at her work, where she ran a busy sales department of twenty people and she was good at it. But, at home she didn't want to be in control. There she wanted to submit to her husband, to do what he wanted and expected of her. Some things they never discussed, such as who would do the chores in their household. Nora wasn't a slave and Edward didn't want her to be one. They shared the household tasks, did the grocery shopping together and discussed destinations for holidays. They always came to mutual decisions. The only thing that Nora had no say about, was her body and sex life. She had handed the control of that over to Edward.

Edward and Nora read a lot about BDSM, but in the end they did things their own way – the way that fitted their life together. Edward trained Nora to be the submissive he wanted, and she gladly followed his lead. There were specific things he wanted her to be ready for. One of his demands was that she needed to be ready and prepared to be fucked by other men. Women too. He wanted to see how other people enjoyed her body because he allowed it. He loved the thought of sharing her with others. Nora had to think it over, but after several months she admitted to Edward that she liked the idea of being used for the pleasure of others. Thoughts of being treated like a slut excited her. They started attending kinky parties to meet other people. In the safe environment of a club they experimented. On their first night visiting a club, Edward bound Nora to a St. Andrew's cross and flogged her back and bottom while other people stood around them. The rest of that night they walked around and observed other couples engaging in different kinds and states of play.

Each time they went out to a club, they took it a step further. Edward allowed other men to whip her and women to touch her. The women sometimes soothed her when her bottom was red and bruised. Other times they frigged her clitoris until she climaxed. Nora got used to being on display and touched by strangers. That first time at the club she was self-conscious and wanted to hide, but she didn't because she wanted Edward to be proud of her. With each time they visited the club, she was more at ease, but the self-consciousness never disappeared. She was conscious of her naked body, aware of Edward watching over her and protecting her. Nora also saw the looks from other men. There was desire in their eyes, but they followed the protocol of the club and kept their distance, unless Edward invited them to take part in flogging or whipping her.

On the last Saturday of every month, the club organized a huge party with events taking place in different rooms. On this particular Saturday, there was an auction in one of the rooms.

"You're ready," Edward said two days before the party.

"Ready for what, Sir?" Nora asked.

"To be used."

Nora knew what he meant. Excitement and fear filled her in equal measures. She didn't know anything of Edward's plans, but she knew better than to ask him. Her safety was always his number one concern. She never had to worry about that and never did. Edward would never let her do anything where he couldn't fully protect her. He would also never leave her alone with anyone else. They were always together. Nora trusted Edward with her life.

Nora received clear instructions from Edward what to wear to the party. Or rather, he told her what not to wear. She wore a dress, stockings and patent leather high-heeled pumps. Everything was black, just the way Edward liked it. Her dress barely covered her ass and didn't hide the top of her lacy hold-up stockings. At the club they roamed around between the different events. They attended a flogging demonstration and another demonstration where a woman had needles stuck into the soft flesh around her nipples. Nora shivered. Needle play was one item she had on her list of hard limits. She found it arousing to look at, but her fear for needles would forever keep her from trying it. Hand in hand they wandered to other rooms, watching and learning. Nora waited patiently for Edward's instructions.

The auction was the main event of the evening. Edward took her to the room adjacent to the big room where the buyers waited for the subjects to be brought onto the stage. Together with others, Nora waited until they called her name. They talked nervously while waiting. Nora learned that the others were a mixture of slaves and submissives – men and women. They were the subjects, waiting to be sold by their owners, to be used by others. Besides being nervous, they were excited too. The first subject disappeared to the big room next door. Through the half opened door Nora heard that the owner auctioned his submissive to be caned by five men for a total of hundred lashes. A shiver ran though her when she heard it and she wondered what Edward had in store for her. One by one the submissives and slaves left the room. Nora heard how one of them was sold to be flogged, another to have her breasts tortured, others to be tied up and suspended in the air. Nora was the last one to be called to the stage.

She opened the door to the next room and walked up the stairs of the makeshift stage. The other subjects stood in a group to one side, waiting to go with the dominants who had bought them. Nora stopped in the middle of the stage and tried to ignore all the faces looking up at her. The auctioneer beckoned her closer. She took another step towards him and stopped again. He grabbed her hand and pulled her closer.

"This fine specimen is auctioned by her master, Sir Edward. What do you think she's auctioned for? No, wait," he held up his hand, "let's see the merchandise first, before I tell you that."

He turned to Nora.

"Please take off your dress."

Nora glanced at Edward and she saw his slight nod. With no further hesitation, she took her dress off and dropped it to the floor. She folded her arms behind her, in the small of her back.

"Now ladies and gentlemen," the auctioneer continued, "here you see a fine specimen. Look at those gorgeous breasts. Firm and round and ready to be touched."

He paused a moment for effect, looked at the buyers from left to right and then back again.

"Turn around, Nora," he said in a matter-of-fact tone as he turned back to her.

Nora turned around, her arms still behind her.

"Hands forward please," the auctioneer requested and Nora obeyed again.

"The back is just as beautiful as the front. Fine round buttocks and the straight back. Truly a fine specimen, ladies and gentlemen. A. Real. Fine. Specimen."
Nora blushed at the words, even though she had heard him say similar things about the men and women who stood on the stage before her.

"Let's see," the auctioneer said as he looked down at the papers he held in his hand. "Ah," he continued, "sorry ladies, this one is only for the men."

Nora's body stiffened in anticipation.

"Ten lucky men will get to fuck this woman tonight. Let's start the bidding at 10 euros."

The low starting point didn't offend Nora, because the auction was for mutual enjoyment and not about the money. Whoever won the auction would choose nine other men to join him in a gang-bang, with Nora as their plaything. Even though bidding started so low, the winning dominant eventually paid 125 euros for Nora. Nora joined the other submissives. It was time for the winners to claim their prizes.

Edward took Nora's hand after she had given him her dress. He pulled her with him. The man who had won her in the auction, waited on the other side of the room. Nine other men stood around him.

"Kneel," Edward said.

Nora did as she was told. She bowed her head and put her hands behind her back. The men discussed rules and limits. She couldn't make out what they said, because of their whispered voices.

"Come," Edward said and held his hand out to her.

They moved on to a room down the hallway. In the middle of the room stood a huge round bed. Edward ordered Nora to take off her stockings and shoes. He took it from her and sat down on a chair in the corner of the room. From there he kept an eye on all proceedings, checking that all the men kept to what they had agreed upon.

The winner of the auction led her to the bed.

"All you have to do is lie here and let it happen," he said and chuckled. "We will do the work."

He swung his arm in a wide circle to include all the other men. Soon everyone was naked. They joined her on the bed. Nora was in the middle and within reach of all the men. Hands touched her all over – her shoulders, her feet, her breasts, her legs and her pussy. Nora was unaware that more people had entered the room. Men guided her hands to cocks on either side of her. A third penis entered her mouth. Two men pulled her legs apart and touched her cunt, spreading her labia and pushing fingers inside her. Nora was wet with excitement. Never had she thought she would enjoy being the center of attention or to be used by men she didn't know. She moved her hands up and down the shafts in her hands and opened her mouth wide for the cock to push in deeper. Nora gasped as a cock pushed deep into her pussy.

She tried to concentrate on every sensation, to separate them in her mind. She wanted to remember how the cocks felt in her hands, in her mouth and in her pussy. Her brain failed to do it. All sensations ran together. Nora surrendered to the feelings. She did what she had been told: she just let it happen.

Between her legs one man moved away, and another took his place. The cock that entered her next was thinner than the previous one, but longer. Over and over the men fucked her. A thick cock and a thin one, a long cock and a short one. Each cock felt different and caused different sensations inside her. The ten men all entered her several times, not shooting their loads. The men changed places often to make them last longer. Nora expected some of the men to climax in her mouth, but that didn't happen either. One man pulled her to the edge of the bed. Her head hung backwards. He shoved his cock deep into her mouth. Slow and deliberate he fucked her mouth. His erection touched the back of her throat and she gagged. Soothing sounds came from the owner of the cock when he pulled back, but not out of her mouth. Nora tried to relax and surprised herself by being able to take more when he pushed in again. Saliva dribbled from her mouth onto her cheeks and into her hair, but for once she didn't care.

Edward looked on with pride as the men used his slutty wife. From where he sat it was obvious that she enjoyed it as much as he did. Nora had several orgasms during the fucking and sucking. She had always been a sexual beast. This was one of her deepest fantasies: to be used and fucked by many men at the same time. He wanted to give her this, but he also wanted to break one of her soft limits today. He was curious to see how she would handle that.

On the bed Nora's pussy ached after the umpteenth time of being filled by a thick, hard penis. She moaned and almost pulled away. This was a clear sign that the men had to draw the fucking to an end. It surprised Nora when all men pulled away from her. Her hands were empty, as were her mouth and her pussy. The men positioned themselves around her. She watched as they all took their hard cocks in their hands. For a moment panic showed in her eyes. This was one of her soft limits: she didn't want men to come on her body. She couldn't see Edward but she instinctively knew that this was his wish. Nora wanted to close her eyes and wait for it all to be over, but she couldn't. There was something so mesmerizing about the men masturbating around her, that it kept her from disappearing into herself. Her hand crept to her clitoris and with her eyes taking in the different expressions on the faces of the men, she masturbated with them. Collectively, they allowed her to have one more orgasm, before they followed. Warm jets of semen hit her body as the men climaxed one after the other. Now Nora closed her eyes. Fluids hit her breasts, her stomach and her face. It ran down her cheeks, into her hair and mixed with her own saliva. The semen was warm as it hit her body, but sticky only moments later as it began to dry.

That night was the start of their encounters involving other people. After the gang-bang, Nora cleaned herself up and re-dressed. They went downstairs to have a drink at the bar, where nudity wasn't allowed. Some of the men whom had just fucked Nora were at the bar, but also several of the spectators. It was only then that Nora learned that the room had been full of people enjoying the show on the round bed. Woman and men came by to congratulate Nora on handling all the men. That was when they met a couple from South Africa. The couple told them how they had met kinky people on social media and heard about the BDSM clubs and dungeons in Europe. They came to the Netherlands for two weeks and would travel on to the United Kingdom for another two weeks before they returned home. The couple invited Edward and Nora for a drink and the four of them ended up in a bar down the street from the BDSM club. They talked through the night and two days later, they met in the visiting couple's hotel room.

Nora got tied up together with the other woman, who was submissive to her husband too. The men whipped and caned the two women, leaving them bruised and tired. No fucking happened that afternoon, but it was not because of lack of interest. After the intense session, the women showered together. There was a mutual attraction between them and both admitted being curious about making love to another woman. However, it couldn't happen that same day, as they had a dinner reservation in the restaurant of the hotel. By the time the South African couple left to go to the United Kingdom, Edward and Nora were invited to visit them on their farm in South Africa. They accepted the invitation, but had to wait until their next big vacation before they could make the trip. Now, less than half a year later, they were excited about the adventures they might have on the secluded farm in the country down south.

In the months before they boarded the plane, their own relationship deepened. They hooked up with more couples. Even though Edward and Nora had great experiences, they didn't have the same connection with any of the other couples than they had with the South Africans. Nora blushed when she admitted to Edward that she was slightly in love with the South African woman. Edward and Nora still visited BDSM clubs and parties, where Nora was frequently used in front of a crowd. Her submission was deeper than it had been when they started their special relationship. Even though she still had her independence inside her marriage with Edward, her submission oozed through in all aspects of their days. They were a happy couple and appreciated by many others in 'the scene'.

Here they were, in their seats on the plane to South Africa. Passengers still boarded the plane, searched for their seats and put their cabin luggage away in the overhead compartments. Edward and Nora both absentmindedly watched the other passengers. Some people looked tense and others joked with their travel companions. Edward noticed a young couple on the other side of the plane, in the seats mirroring that of him and Nora. The two were all over each other, holding hands and kissing. He turned his head towards his wife. Her hands were still in her lap, the palms turned upward. She wore her shiny collar with pride. It looked like a regular piece of jewelry, but he had it made for her on special order. Only people who knew more about dominance and submission would recognize it as a day collar and a symbol of being owned. If people read the inscription on the inside, they would suspect that there was a deeper meaning to it: *You are MINE. Forever.*

Edward's thoughts jumped a couple of hours ahead to that evening and their first night on the farm of their friends. He and his friend abroad had discussed this at length. During their sexy encounters while the South African couple was still in the Netherlands, the two men were aware that the women wanted more. Neither of them dared to step out of line with their husbands and owners. That night it would change. The women would be locked up in a room and given carte blanche. Several cameras would film them from different angles. The men would see everything that happened inside the room. Edward smiled, leaned over towards Nora and kissed her on the cheek.

"Try to get some sleep during the flight," he said, "there's a slight possibility you will get little sleep tonight."

Butterflies stirred in Nora's stomach as she smiled up at him.

Chapter Six
Recovering the victims

Sounds of sirens filled the air as emergency vehicles drew closer to the wreckage of the crashed plane. Only the blue and red lights remained as the noise stopped. People spilled from the insides of the cars and trucks and started emergency procedures. Their first priority was to look for survivors, but before they could do that, the fire teams had to put out the fires. The smoldering was soon dampened down and the remaining kerosene in the fuel tanks made safe. Once the firemen had done their part, the teams of emergency workers moved in.

In five teams they worked the crash site – two teams from the back of the plane, one on each side and two teams from the front, also one on each side. A fifth team checked for safety before they entered the front and the back parts of the plane. The part of the aircraft behind the wings had broken into pieces. The tailpiece was intact, as was the cockpit, the business class area and part of the economic class. Each member of the teams wore a hard hat, with a light on it to illuminate their own way. It was pitch-dark out in the desert and the coastal road had no lights. Neither were there any lights on inside the plane. On their first scan the emergency people found no survivors. A more intense search started as soon as more emergency workers arrived.

The teams checked each body for vital signs. They were quiet as they moved along and listened for sounds, but all they heard was the gentle lapping of the waves at the beach. Poignant scenes unfolded in front of them: a mother still holding her son's hand, a man with his arms in a protective embrace around the woman next to him; two women holding hands, facing each other and hanging in their seats; a man with his arms in front of his face as if to hide the horrific scene around him. These people almost seemed like they had frozen in their positions with the plane's impact. Not all bodies were intact. Some missed a leg or an arm. Or more. There was blood everywhere, but some victims had no blood on them at all.

In the meantime, while the members of the emergency teams worked, the response team leader – Captain Clarke – contacted the airports in Amsterdam and Johannesburg. He confirmed that Flight LU-365 had crashed between Swakopmund and Walvis Bay with 303 people on board. It was unclear why the aircraft crashed at this location, because the flying route didn't come close to this area. The direction from where the plane seemed to have crashed was wrong too. It flew in from the Atlantic Ocean, but the flight path should not have taken it over the Atlantic Ocean or Namibia. Captain Clarke listened as the air traffic control officer in Windhoek informed him of further actions.

"A team of investigators will board a plane in Amsterdam tonight. They will arrive in Windhoek tomorrow morning. From there they will fly on to Walvis Bay and arrive at the crash site by the end of the day tomorrow. Another team of investigators will fly in from Johannesburg," the voice in the phone told the team leader.

Before he could ask anything, the voice continued: "To get a quick start to the crash investigation, a preliminary team from Windhoek is already on their way to Walvis Bay."

Captain Clarke received specific instructions to make snapshots of everything they saw, including the victims. Only when a first series of images had been taken, the emergency teams could move the deceased from the scene.

When no survivors were found, the emergency teams reported back to the team leader, who gave them instructions on what to do next.

"I want you to divide into four teams. Each team will work a quarter of the crash site. Take photos, people, take photos! Make sure you take enough before you move anything. Even more so since it's dark."

Photos were necessary to give a full report of exactly where each body had been found, in relation to pieces of the wreck.

"You are better off taking too many photos than not enough," Captain Clarke emphasized, "Tag each body with the number of the section you're working."

Four team captains were appointed and each team captain got a notebook to write down everything they saw, smelled or thought was necessary to bring to the attention of the air crash investigators. Everyone knew that they wouldn't sleep much for several days, and definitely not at all in the coming hours. A lot of work needed to be done in the next couple of days, with the main goal to get the deceased back to their loved ones for burial. This, however, couldn't happen until the victims had been examined by medical professionals. As the teams got back to work, Captain Clarke called different undertakers in Swakopmund and Walvis Bay and asked them to send their hearses out to the crash scene.

"Please keep the news about the plane crash quiet. We want to keep curious onlookers and reporters away from the scene as long as possible," he told the different undertakers.

Not one undertaker refused to drive to the crash site. They would have to drive on and off to get all the victims to the two towns. There was nothing else the chief could do other than to supervise the progress of recovering the victims of the crash. The teams had started to lay the corpses in rows several meters away from the plane and away from the debris of the crash. Their work was difficult because of the dark. They only had the lights on their hard hats to light their ways. Even so, it was a sad sight to see the dead bodies next to each other, with nothing to cover them. There were not enough white sheets or body bags available. They had to wait for the first hearses to arrive.

Captain Clarke shook his head as he walked down the line of victims, knowing that this was only the beginning. So much more work had to be done before all the victims would be identified and returned to their next of kin. Hearses arrived from both towns. The process of moving bodies from the crash site could start. They ran into the problem that there was no mortuary in Swakopmund and all victims had to be taken to Walvis Bay. There was no way to get the hearses from Swakopmund to drive to Walvis Bay, because the crashed plane blocked the road. It would take days, possibly weeks, before the road would be open for traffic again.

The team leader called the military base in Walvis Bay and arranged for an improvised mortuary where all victims could be taken.

"I have already sent several vehicles your way," the commander of the military base informed Captain Clarke, "Air traffic control in Windhoek called and asked for the military's assistance."

While discussing the situation, the commander suggested to detour the road between Swakopmund and Walvis Bay into the desert using pontoons. If the wreck was here for weeks, there would be no way for people who lived in the one town and worked in the other to get where they needed to be.

Captain Clarke was barely done with the phone call when he saw the lights and then heard the roar of the big military trucks approaching from Walvis Bay. It was too dark to see the trucks until they stopped behind the emergency vehicles, switched off their lights and were illuminated by the flashing lights. The army had arrived. Without disturbing the crash site and with trained precision, the soldiers started to work. They placed power generators on the border of the crash site and connected wires to it. Stands with huge lights appeared from the trucks. Within an hour after the five military trucks had pulled up to the crash site, the entire area flooded with light. Suddenly the tragedy was all that clearer. Lumps formed in big men's throats. The dignity of the aircraft was gone as it lay there, broken and disgraceful. The eerie sight of the broken wings and intact nose sticking up in the air humbled the people below. Huge tears in the body of the plane resembled giant open mouths.

The teams worked and hearses drove to and from Walvis Bay throughout the night. The undertakers from Swakopmund helped to get the victims into the hearses from Walvis Bay. As soon as the military personnel had the pontoons in place, the Swakopmund hearses could drive to Walvis Bay too. An army truck joined the hearses in transporting the victims. They wanted to get the bigger part of the bodies from the scene before the break of dawn in the desert and before the hearses drew too much attention from people along the way. It was a painstakingly slow operation. Just before the daybreak, more trucks arrived, this time with the pontoons. The soldiers worked on a detour for the coastal road. The detour would take the traffic into the desert and around the dunes, to keep the crash site shielded from view. Just outside Swakopmund and Walvis Bay traffic cops blocked the road. Traffic would only be allowed on the coastal road again once the detour was ready to be used.

It took well into the afternoon before the detoured road was ready. By then all the victims outside the plane had been transported to the improvised mortuary in the military base of Walvis Bay. Getting victims from inside the plane was more difficult and a longer process. Only one small team could work inside the plane and victims had to be taken out one by one. Before they could be removed from their seats, the deceased had to be photographed and tagged. Next, the victim was placed in a rescue stretcher, the same kind used in the mountains when an injured climber needed to be transported. Rescue workers then formed a line and the stretcher was carefully lowered to the ground, where a second team of rescue workers waited to take the victim to a hearse or the army truck for transport to Walvis Bay.

While the emergency teams worked to get all the victims out and the military worked to get the detour of the road organized, another team of military men put up several tents. One tent became the kitchen and mess, and five other tents were designated to be the sleeping quarters for the emergency workers. Shifts were organized. Emergency workers didn't want to leave until all victims were salvaged, but they needed to rest. None of them slept for more than three hours before they were back on the job again. Forty-seven hours after the first emergency vehicles arrived at the scene, the pilot and his co-pilot were the last victims to be removed from the scene. Only the empty plane and the surrounding wreckage remained.

Early in the evening on the day after the crash, the air crash investigation teams arrived from Windhoek. The army put up another tent for them to use as an operation center, equipped with communication devices to keep in contact with the international airports in Amsterdam, Johannesburg and Windhoek. Not long after the investigation teams arrived, the first traffic appeared on the detoured pontoon road. Police guarded the road on the other side of the dunes from the crash site, making sure no one pulled over and climbed up the dune to see something of the crash site.

After all the victims were salvaged and taken to the mortuary in the military base, the emergency people left the crash site. Only Captain Clarke and three police officers from Swakopmund remained at the scene to aid the air crash investigation team.

The investigation to find the cause of the crash started.

Chapter Seven
Joe and Mattie

Joe and Mattie were madly in love, but they didn't display their love as openly as newlywed couples normally did. They weren't young people anymore. Joe was sixty-seven, Mattie sixty-five and both of them were retired.

Joe had worked as a service operator for a chocolate factory for most of his adult working years. He was married before, to the mother of his four children. She died two years before he retired. They had so many plans for trips they wanted to make once he was retired and had saved up enough money to make it possible. Joe's three sons and one daughter were all married and had their own families. Joe had six grandchildren. Two of his sons had two sons each, his youngest son had a daughter and his daughter had a son. They spent birthdays and all festive days together at Joe's place. He loved having his children and grandchildren around him. Days were busy when they were all there, but being surrounded by love was never a bad thing in Joe's book.

When Joe's wife was still alive, she always took care of the cooking and baking, making sure everyone had more than enough. After her passing, their daughter took this task on her. Joe's daughters-in-law helped too, but his own daughter always took charge of all arrangements. He appreciated that nothing changed after his wife's death. He had mourned her, but Joe lived from day to day and he was happy with his life as it was. Joe had a lot of savings, but there was nothing he wanted to use it for. He couldn't fulfill his dream anymore to go on trips abroad with his wife. His children would have to share his savings when he passed. Joe wasn't looking for a life partner. His life was full and rich and he was content.

Joe kept busy by making wooden furniture. He did this at his own leisure and once he finished a piece, he put it up for sale. He wasn't into it for the money, but for being able to create things with his hands. Joe made furniture for grown-ups, but also toys for kids. His grandchildren all owned several pieces that 'Gramps Joe' had made. There was the furniture for his granddaughter's dollhouse, but also the wooden cars and carts for his grandsons. Joe had made each of the grandchildren a small chair with their names carved in the backrests.

One day, Joe received a call from a friend who asked him if he could make a small dinner table for one of his female acquaintances. Joe didn't like working on order, but out of politeness asked how big the table should be and whether he would need to make matching chairs too. Chairs weren't necessary and the table would have to be big enough for two people and preferably square. Since the table didn't have to be that big and Joe was in-between projects, he decided to take on the job.

Joe needed to know the exact measurements for the table. Instead of asking his friend for this information, he asked for the woman's telephone number so he could call her to make an appointment. Several days later he rang the bell to her apartment. Joe was temporary shocked into silence when she opened the door. The woman in front of him was approximately his age. Her appearance blew his mind. She was beautiful with her silver gray hair and sparkling blue eyes. Despite her age, the skin on her face was smooth and well taken care of, as was the skin on her soft hands. She was immaculately dressed, but not in an 'old woman' way.

"I'm... er... uh... I'm... uh..." Joe stuttered.

"You're Joe," the woman said, "and you're here for the table. I'm Mattie. Please come in," she said in a soft and friendly voice.

Joe stepped inside. He was immediately in awe of this woman. There was something in her demeanor that attracted him in a way he couldn't resist. He didn't want to resist it. In fact, he was so blown away that he forgot about the table. He wanted to get to know her. For the first time since his wife died four years earlier, a woman awakened his interest again.

Even though Mattie appeared to be confident when she invited Joe into her home, she wasn't. For the first time in years, she had butterflies in her stomach.

She noticed the way Joe looked at her and instantly recognized it as being more than just general interest. It flattered her that he seemed to be overwhelmed enough to stutter, but it did nothing to quiet down the excited butterflies. Thankfully, she knew how to hide her shaking hands and the fact that she was just as taken aback as Joe was: tea. Tea was always the solution! She ushered him to the living room and told him she would make them some tea. Neither she, nor Joe noticed that she didn't even check whether he liked tea. In the kitchen she busied herself with putting cups and saucers on a tray and teaspoons on the saucers next to the cups. She put biscuits on a separate plate and the plate onto a tray and a small sugar bowl and a tiny milk jug joined the rest. By then the water boiled. She put a tea bag into the teapot that matched the sugar bowl and milk jug, poured water in it and put the lid on. Mattie took the tray to the living room where Joe sat in a chair, wringing his hands together.

Mattie smiled at him and put the tray on the small round table between the two armchairs. Joe sat right on the edge of one of the two armchairs, his elbows resting on the armrests. He rubbed his hands and wrung them together as if washing them. Mattie still smiled, secretly enjoying the effect she seemed to have on him. This surprised her. She was unfamiliar with this side of her personality. Under different circumstances, she would chatter away and put a person at ease with her talking, but she couldn't find any words. Mattie busied her hands with the tea, pouring each of them a cup.

"Do you take sugar?" she asked Joe.

"Sugar, no milk, thanks," Joe said, and he was grateful to take the cup from her. He needed something in his hands to keep them still. Mattie poured milk in her tea before she held the plate with cookies out to him. Joe ate a biscuit and emptied his cup of tea in one gulp. He looked at Mattie and remembered why he was there.

"So, you want a table?" he asked.

"Yes, I want a small table where I can have my meals," Mattie answered.

"Where do you want it?"

Joe looked around the room as he waited for Mattie's answer. He saw no space for a table, no matter how small he made it. Maybe she wanted it in the kitchen? However, Mattie explained that the showcase would be moved to her daughter's place and then that corner of the room would become the dining area. She had no other space for a table, but she was tired of having her meals on a tray on her knees. Joe stood up and retrieved the tape measure from his back pocket. He walked to the corner she indicated and took the measurements.

"Shall I pour us more tea while you're busy?" Mattie asked and Joe nodded. He was done in a few minutes and when he sat down again, Mattie passed him his cup of tea.

"So, what's the verdict?" she asked.

"Huh?" Joe looked at her, not understanding what she meant.

"Can you make me a table?"

"Ah!" Joe laughed, "of course I can. I can make you anything you want. But I guess you want to know whether I can make a table that fits there?"

That was the icebreaker. Joe and Mattie soon talked about other things than the table. Both of them forgot the real reason for Joe's visit. They talked about their lives, where they grew up, where they went to school, where they met their first partners and how their partners died. They told each other about their children, their grandchildren and about what kept them busy in their daily lives. Joe learned that Mattie was the same age his wife would have been if she was still alive. Mattie had been a widow for just more than nine years. Her husband died in a car accident on his way to his work one morning. He was a construction worker and fell asleep while driving. He drove into the canal along which he had to drive to his work. No one saw the accident, because it was dark and there were no other cars on the road that early. His boss called Mattie when her husband didn't get to work on time. She called the emergency services. By then the driver of another car had spotted the roof of her husband's car in the canal. It was too late to save him.

Mattie had two children – a son and a daughter. Her daughter had two daughters and her son had no children. He and his wife didn't want children. Mattie told Joe about her family. She saw her daughter frequently, but her son and his wife traveled all over the world for their jobs and they visit at irregular times. Mattie loved to have her children and grandchildren around her. Happiness filled Joe's heart when he realized they had that in common. He shook his head and scolded himself: *don't be a silly old man! You're only here for the table!*

He glanced at his watch and jumped up.

"I am so sorry," he apologized profusely, "I haven't seen the time!"

He had left home just after he had lunch and now his watch told him it was time to prepare his dinner. He had been with Mattie for hours!

"I don't mind. I enjoyed your visit," Mattie said with a sweet smile.

Joe was back to wringing his hands. This woman touched him in a way that no woman had since his wife died. He quickly gave her a hand and disappeared through the door.

Making the table for Mattie was his first labor of love for her. Joe couldn't get her out of his mind. Her eyes haunted him, but in a nice way. He could constantly hear her voice in his ears, even though two weeks passed before he saw her again. Her smile followed him everywhere. He played their conversation of that afternoon in his mind over and over again. By the time he completed the table, Joe admitted to himself: *I'm in love.* It felt awkward. Falling in love again had been so far from his mind that he never took into account it might happen. How did he have to do this? How should he tell Mattie about his feelings? He didn't even know *if* he should tell her about it. Things were so much easier when he was younger!

Joe waited a week before he contacted Mattie. He tried to sound matter-of-fact over the telephone. They agreed on a date for the delivery of the table. He was like a teenager after the short conversation with her. Hearing her voice had called up her face in his mind and if he even was in doubt, it confirmed his feelings for her.

Three days later he rang the bell of Mattie's apartment again. The door opened even before the chiming of the bell died down. Mattie stood there with a huge smile on her face, just as happy to see Joe again as he was to be there. She invited him in.

"I will be with you in a moment," she said as Joe walked through to the sitting room.

Joe was more relaxed than the first time. Seeing Mattie again confirmed his suspicions: what had happened the first time he saw her, was love on first sight. All he needed now was a way to tell her about his feelings. He had prepared himself for a disappointment, but seeing Mattie and the way she acted towards him, he suspected she felt the same about him. Mattie walked in with a tray in her hands. The same set of cups, saucers, teapot, sugar bowl and milk jug were on the tray. This time she didn't have cookies on a plate, but a freshly baked cake. Joe instantly recognized it as homemade and not bought at a bakery or supermarket.

Joe took a bite of his cake and complimented Mattie on the taste.

"I baked it for you," she said and Joe smiled when a blush covered her face.

"That's nice, but you didn't do this especially for me, did you?" he teased.

"Yes, I did," she admitted and her face turned a deeper red.

"But why?"

Mattie just looked at him and smiled. Joe didn't see an old woman in front of him. He saw a beautiful girl flirting with him; a woman trying to tell him something with her eyes. Joe smiled, leaned forward and took her hand in his. Her hand was soft and warm and she didn't pull back.

"Mattie," Joe said, deciding to just go ahead and say it. At their age there was no time to spill, no time to dance around each other for months without admitting true feelings. Life was literally too short.

"Mattie," he said again, "I could not stop thinking of you since I was here the last time."

"But, why not, Joe?" Mattie asked coquettishly and even though she was halfway through her sixties, yet again she looked like a young woman to Joe.

"I think I fell for you the first time," Joe admitted and held his breath.

"You fell?" Mattie joked, "I didn't notice."

She saw the confusion on Joe's face and quickly continued: "Sorry, sometimes I'm a bit shy and then I make lame jokes. I fell too, Joe. For you. You were in my thoughts day and night from the moment you left here the last time."

Joe's chest swelled with love and pride and happiness. On impulse, he leaned closer to Mattie and kissed her on her cheek.

"I'm so happy," he said and Mattie nodded in full agreement.

They were quiet for a while, enjoying a second cup of tea, that Mattie had poured to calm her own excitement. They constantly glanced at each other, smiled and then looked away, only to look back at each other again.

The two of them talked about a lot of things that afternoon. In the past two weeks they hadn't only thought about each other, but also about how they would tell their children they were in love. Another thought was what kind of relationship they wanted. Would they want to live together or would each of them want to maintain a part of their own independence by living apart and having a modern long distance relationship? They were in quick agreement. If they engaged in a relationship, in time they wanted to live together under one roof. They were still old-fashioned enough to want to be together as husband and wife. Their first priority was to get to know each other better in the next couple of weeks. If they still felt the same after spending a lot of time together, the next priority would be to tell their children. It was hours later that Joe left to go home. By then the table was in Mattie's home and he had helped her to create a nice and cozy corner where she could have her meals from then on.

Joe was insanely happy. He would see Mattie again in a couple of days, but before that he had a dinner to attend at his daughter's place. At home Joe started on a new project: two chairs to match Mattie's new table. She planned to use a stool to sit on when she had her meals, but he wanted her to be comfortable and he wanted to share some of her meals with her. The two chairs would be his surprise for her. Joe sang and whistled all the time while he worked. Nothing could get him in a bad mood. It wasn't like he actually had bad moods, but his mood was extremely positive since his last visit to Mattie. The knowledge that she was in love with him too, made his heart sing. He arrived at his daughter's place two hours before dinnertime, just like he always did. He spent time with his grandson and then with his daughter in the kitchen while she cooked dinner. Several times he saw her glancing at him in a strange way. She did the same at the dinner table and yet again after she had put her son to bed.

"What's going on, Dad?" she asked.

"What's going on with what?" Joe asked, not understanding her question.

"Who is she?" his daughter smiled.

"How did you know?" Joe answered her with a question of his own.

"You are different. Happier. You sing. You whistle. I haven't heard that since mom died," his daughter explained with a loving smile.

"Would you mind if there is a 'she' in my life?" Joe asked.

His stomach tightened as he waited for her answer.

"Oh Dad, no, of course not," she laughed, "we talked about it a lot when you weren't around. We would love it if you have someone special for yourself again. You deserve to be loved again."

She stood up to hug him and went to the kitchen to make them coffee. Joe stayed behind, staring out in front of him and thinking how wonderful his children were. He hoped that Mattie's children would accept a new man in their mom's life as willingly as his children accepted a new woman in his.

It was written in the stars that they would be together. Joe was convinced of this when he visited Mattie again. Since the last time they had seen each other,

Mattie had invited her children over for tea. Just like Joe's daughter intuitively knew that her father was in love, both Mattie's children knew that their mom had something important to share for her to invite them both. She was adamant that they had to come together. Mattie's children thought their mom would tell them she was seriously sick. The moment she opened the door and they saw the twinkle in her eyes and the smile on her face, they knew: their mom was in love. Relief flooded through them and they found themselves instantly and unconditionally happy for their mom, even before she said one word about her newfound happiness. Joe was ecstatic when he learned that none of their children would stand in the way of their happiness.

In the next months, Joe and Mattie got to know each other better, and met each other's children and grandchildren. Since Mattie lived in a small apartment, all gatherings happened at Joe's house, which was big enough to host everyone. They celebrated birthdays there, hosted several dinner parties together and it didn't take that long before Mattie barely slept in her own bed anymore. Since Joe and Mattie were in the autumn of their lives, they wanted to be together as much as possible. They were still healthy and both of them had a healthy interest in sex. Nevertheless, their first time was awkward and almost like they never had sex before. They were clumsy when they lay together in bed for the first time. They bumped their foreheads when they wanted to kiss and fumbled with each other's pajamas so much that they giggled childishly by the time they were naked at last.

Joe looked at Mattie's naked body in the low light of the bedside lamp. The history of her life was written on her body. There was a scar on her tummy from an operation combined with faded stretch marks from her two pregnancies. Her breasts were not firm anymore and gray highlights showed in her pubic hair.

"You are simply beautiful," he said as he bent down to kiss her.

Mattie's arms went around Joe's muscular body. Had she not known he was older than her, she would have thought she had a young hunk in her arms. The mere thought made her blush. His furniture-making hobby sure kept his body in shape. She ran her hands down to his buttocks and those were firm too. Between them, his cock pressed against her leg. She shivered with delight.

"Are you cold?" Joe asked.

"No," she smiled and giggled like a teenager, "I'm horny."

"Now then," Joe said with a grin, "let's see what we can do about that."

Mattie thought he would fuck her, but instead he slipped his fingers into her.

"You first," he said, "then me. I'm an old man, you know!"

Mattie understood. Joe's fingers moved in and out of her in a steady pace. Her orgasm built slowly. It had been years since her last orgasm by the hands of a man and it didn't surprise her that it took longer. But, she could still reach an orgasm and she did. Joe kissed her.

"Thank you," Mattie said and hugged him.

He mounted her and slipped his cock inside her. It didn't take him long to climax. Mattie had understood it correctly: age had gotten to both of them. Still, she was confident they would have a good sex life. She loved the kindness of Joe attending first to her needs, before his own. They fell asleep holding hands. The next morning, they made love again.

Joe and Mattie were inseparable. They knew their time together would never be as long as the time they had with their first partners. Just ten months into their relationship, Joe asked Mattie to marry him. After lunch, they sat together at the small table he had made for her. Mattie had just poured them each a cup of coffee, when Joe took both her hands in his and looked at her with a serious expression on his face. She instinctively knew what words would follow.

"Mattie, will you marry me?"
"Yes! Yes, I will, Joe!"

She answered almost before he asked the question. Joe kissed her softly on her lips. Excitement filled the air as they talked about how they would do it, where they wanted to be married, when to tell the children, whether they wanted to have a honeymoon and if so, where they wanted to go. They also had to decide whether they wanted a new house or if the one would move in with the other.

They told the children that weekend. It was late summer and the weather was good enough to have a barbecue in Joe's back garden. All their children and grandchildren were invited. Right after dinner Joe rounded everyone up in his living room. Some of them sat in the two couches, other stood behind the couches or around Joe and Mattie. Joe held his arm around his soon-to-be wife's shoulders. He cleared his throat and looked at Mattie.

"As you all know, Mattie and I have been together for close to a year now. We want to be together every day. Since we don't know how much time we have left and we want to do that sooner rather than later, I have asked Mattie to marry me and she has accepted."

He waited for the protests. There was only silence. Joe didn't dare taking his eyes off Mattie to look at their children. Mattie kept her eyes fixed on his face too, waiting for the reactions. The silence lasted for a long three seconds before the applause started. Joe and Mattie looked at their children with love and surprise. There were smiles all around and all the children clapped their hands. Even the little ones clapped along, though they didn't know the reason for it. The love and happiness in the room enveloped all of them. Joe turned to Mattie and saw the tears in his own eyes mirrored in hers. He pulled her closer and hugged her tight to his chest.

"I love you," he whispered before he let her go and they accepted hugs, kisses and congratulations from their children.

In the coming weeks Mattie moved in with Joe. Some of her furniture replaced furniture in Joe's house. Either it was pieces she didn't want or they were due to be replaced. The small table and chairs that Joe had made for her and that was symbolic to the start of their love, received a special place in their kitchen. They called it their 'breakfast corner'.

Joe and Mattie had decided that she would give up her apartment. It was too small to house all their children and grandchildren during festivities and it didn't have a garden. Mattie had never lived in that apartment with her late husband, but she knew that Joe's first wife had decorated the house she would move into. She changed a couple of things to her own taste, but did it in such a way that it didn't upset Joe's children. Their bedroom changed and in the living room she replaced some of the decorations with her own. By the time they were done, she was happy and content in her new home without feeling like she would live in the shadow of Joe's first wife. Joe's children were happy too. They expected her to change a lot more and actually encouraged her to do so, but she assured them it was good the way it was.

Now that Mattie was living with Joe, it was time for them to plan their wedding day and honeymoon. Neither of them wanted a huge happening when they got married, but with all their children, grandchildren and some close friends attending, it turned out to be a bigger occasion. Joe and Mattie married in the local town hall. Joe wore a gray suit, white shirt and a burgundy colored tie. Black shoes and burgundy colored socks completed the picture. Mattie looked beautiful in a light pink dress with long lace sleeves. Her shoes perfectly matched the color of her dress and on her head she wore an informal hat that was draped with the same lace she had in her dress. Joe and Mattie looked stunning together. Their love radiated and filled the hearts of all of those around them.

That evening they dined and danced together as husband and wife for the first time. Their children surrounded them and witnessed their first marital kiss, their first marital dance and their obvious love and happiness. Their feet hurt when they arrived home after a lovely evening of celebrating their wedding. For the first time they lay together in bed and made love as husband and wife. They felt like two young people who had their entire life together ahead of them.

The next day the packing for their honeymoon started. While planning their wedding, they also talked about their honeymoon. Joe and Mattie were realistic about their age and that they should make a trip of a lifetime while they could still do so in reasonable health. They chose to go to South Africa. It was the one country they both found fascinating and wanted to visit. Once they landed in Johannesburg, their adventure of eight weeks would start by boarding a touring bus. The trip would take them to various wild parks, under which the well-known Kruger Wild Park, but they would also visit Cape Town to take a trip up Table Mountain, drive along the Garden Route to visit Mossel Bay, Knysna and Port Elizabeth. The Addo Elephant Park was another wild park on the traveling schedule. Joe and Mattie were excited about this trip. It would be their first and last trip outside of Europe.

Early on the morning of the third day after their wedding, Joe and Mattie were ready to leave for their honeymoon. The previous evening all the kids had visited them on and off, to give them kisses and wish them a wonderful honeymoon. Joe's oldest son drove them to the airport, a drive of just more than an hour, and accompanied them to the desk where they checked in. Once their suitcases were on the conveyor belt and they had their boarding passes, Joe and Mattie joined Joe's son for a cup of coffee in a restaurant nearby. Their coffee cups were still hot when they stood up to leave. Joe and Mattie were both nervous. They wanted to get to the gate, to make sure they boarded the plane on time. They both hugged Joe's son and waved at him once more after they passed through customs.

Chapter Eight
Chris and Sarah

They stared at each other. What? Did they really hear it right? Two million? Two million euros?

"Congratulations," the cigarette shop owner said again, "you've won two million euros in the national lottery."

Chris and Sarah couldn't begin to imagine how much money that was or what they could do with it. They were the only customers in the shop at that moment, but even so the owner had taken them to the far corner of the shop. He was discreet about their prize.

"Just a word of advice," he said, "tell no one about your winnings. I've heard horror stories about friends, family, companies and sometimes even complete strangers making a nuisance of themselves when they hear about a prize like this."

Chris nodded. He had heard the same and planned not to tell anyone. By now, his mind already worked overtime: *There are so many ways I can invest this money. Sara and I will have nest egg for later.*

Still dazed, they returned home. Chris and Sarah had no children. In the beginning of their marriage, they tried for Sarah to get pregnant, but when years into their marriage they were still childless, they gave up. They talked about it on various occasions, whether they should go to the doctor and try to find out why Sarah couldn't conceive. Eventually they decided that neither of them wanted to have the medical rigmarole it would cause. If they were meant to have kids, Sarah would have conceived. Since she didn't, they accepted that they would stay childless. That was the firm belief they lived by and it helped them to accept their fate. Chris and Sarah filled their lives with their work and hobbies. Chris worked as a car mechanic on the other side of town and Sarah was a nurse at the local hospital. They both earned a moderate salary and besides their jobs, both kept busy with a hobby. Chris collected stamps and frequently went to trade shows to sell and exchange stamps. Sarah visited the crafts club once a week. She used one room in their house as her work room, where she had an easel and canvases, and different kinds of materials to create whatever her heart desired.

"What shall we do with the money?" Sarah asked.

"I want to invest it," Chris said. "If we invest it, we will have money for our old age."

"Yes," Sarah said, "that's true."

She stared at the tablecloth and traced the lines of the pattern on it with her finger.

"Spill it, puppet!" Chris said, using his pet name for her. He knew that face, the one she always put up when she had something on her mind.

"I would love to make a trip. We've never had money for a trip overseas. We've never been on a real holiday. I don't mind if you invest the money, but please can we make a trip first?"

The words spilled from her mouth in staccato tempo because she was nervous that Chris might deny her this opportunity.

"Where do you want to go?" Chris asked.

"South Africa," Sarah answered in a small voice.

"Okay."

"But, I really want to..." Sarah protested and then realized that Chris had agreed. She stopped and stared at him.

"You mean we can go?" she asked.

"Yes, let's book a vacation to South Africa. I think we deserve that, don't you?"

Sarah was ecstatic with happiness. It had been a dream of her for so long to visit the beautiful country in the most southern tip of Africa. They never had the money for it. That evening she started the search on the World Wide Web to find trips to South Africa. By the time they went to bed, her excitement kept her from falling asleep. She told Chris about things she had found. Her excitement was contagious. Soon he rolled over towards her and kissed her. Their lovemaking followed the same pattern it did for many years. First, they kissed and Chris fondled her breasts. Careful not to hurt her, he lightly kneaded the flesh of her breast in his hand. Next his hand moved down to her crotch, pushing his hand into her pajama bottoms. He cupped her sex and then moved his hand up and down, rubbing her sex. When he thought it was enough, he pushed his finger between her labia. By then she was wet. He pushed her pajama bottoms down, took off his own and rolled over on top of her. Sarah kicked her pajama bottoms off and spread her legs for him, guiding him into her and holding onto his hips. Chris pushed in and out of her several times and when it sounded like she had an orgasm, he picked up the pace until he had his own.

Sarah didn't always climax, but she didn't know any better. In fact, Sarah didn't *think* she ever had a real climax. What she felt at times, *might* be a climax, but she just didn't know. Still, Sarah never had the feeling she was missing out on something. She was content with their sex life the way it was, and so was Chris. Recently, Sarah had read a book about an unconventional love between a rich man and a virgin woman. The book had taken the world by storm and that made her curious to read it too. The plot intrigued her. It stirred up a strange longing in her loins, but the book was fiction and it was ridiculous to think that those things happened in real life. Chris would declare her a fool if she ever suggested for him to give her a spanking, like the dominant man in the book gave the young woman. That was one scene in the book that left Sarah wet and panting.

Chris was just as content with his sex life as his wife was. He had never told Sarah that on the evenings she went out to the craft club, he read the same book she did. Reading about how the rich man dominated that so-called innocent young woman gave him an erection. His favorite part of the book was where the man took the woman into his playroom and bound her wrists and ankles to the bed before he fucked her.

Chris would love to do that to Sarah. He imagined her helpless in front of him, while he did things to her she never imagined might happen. However, he knew if he would tell Sarah about these dark desires, she would tell him to stop being silly and act like the adult he was.

Neither of them knew about the desires of the other. They never talked about their sex life anymore. They talked about a lot of things – their work, their hobbies, their parents, their friends. Chris and Sarah were both happy and content with the way things were. Those hidden desires remained, but they would never tell the other about those silly thoughts.

The next day was a Sunday. Sarah spent all day to continue her search online for their trip to South Africa. She wanted to see and experience so many things. Chris smiled when he saw his wife happily busy planning their trip. She jotted down several pieces of information in a notebook – about wildlife parks, hotels where they could stay or places where they could rent cars. He knew he could leave it to her to plan a lovely trip and even save them money too. Not that money was a problem at that moment, but the more they had left after the trip, the more he could invest for when they retired. Chris was right. Sarah was planning a great trip for them. She plotted out the route. They would fly to Johannesburg, sleep in the airport hotel the first night and rent a car at the airport the next day. From Johannesburg they would drive down to Durban and stay overnight in Harrismith. After two days in Durban, their trip would take them along the coast to Cape Town. Sarah tried to work out how many kilometers they could drive on one day, without rushing it. She jotted down the names of hotels along the way. By the time they went to bed that night, she had a lot of information but she planned to continue her search the next day, when she returned from work.

Sarah surprised Chris when she snuggled close to him again that night. They never had sex more than once a week, but Sarah was in the mood again. Her hand sneaked up to his lower abdomen. He knew what that meant. She wanted him to fuck her. Again, the same routine as always followed... he rolled her over on her back and they kissed. Chris fondled her breasts, careful not to hurt her. He lightly kneaded the flesh of her breast in his hand, before his hand moved down to her crotch, pushing his hand into her pajama bottoms. He cupped her sex and then moved his hand up and down, rubbing her sex. Once she seemed to be wet, he checked by pushing a finger between her labia. She was ready. He pushed her pajama bottoms down, took off his own pajama bottoms and rolled over on top of her. Sarah spread her legs. She guided him into her and held his hips while he moved in and out of her several times before he climaxed. She didn't reach a climax but rolled over to sleep, feeling content and happy with their familiar routine.

Chris enjoyed seeing Sarah happy while she made notes, looked through brochures she had picked up from the travel agency, searched for information on the internet, compared prizes of flight tickets and hotels and checked whether it would be cheaper to go on an organized tour or to drive themselves to the places they wanted to see. Money for the trip wasn't a problem anymore, but Sarah was so used to being careful with their money that she applied the same care to planning the trip. By the end of the week she had it planned out. The only thing that still had to happen was for her and Chris to check with their bosses whether they could have four weeks off from work. They decided not to tell their bosses or colleagues about the money they had won. If anyone asked where they got the money from to make the trip, they would say they had saved to make this happen. Chris and Sarah still kept their winnings a secret, not wanting to have to fend off the vultures at their front door.

It seemed like the universe was granting them this trip just as much as they wanted to make it. Both of them received the green light from their employers to take four weeks off from work. They were ecstatic, so much so that it resulted in another week of making love twice. Sarah surprised Chris by being more passionate than normal during their lovemaking. While he was in her, looking at her as he fucked her, she moved her hand in between them and rubbed her clitoris. She shut her eyes tight and breathed in and out hard through her opened mouth when she climaxed. She caught Chris off-guard when her cunt muscles contracted around him. He stopped moving for a moment, as if to understand what had just happened, before he thrust in her again and reached his own climax. Sarah snuggled close to him afterwards, kissed him on the cheek and said: "I'm happy."

For the first time in many years she fell asleep in his arms.

In the weeks before their trip to South Africa, Sarah never stopped planning. She wanted everything to be perfect for their trip. Sarah checked what clothes they should take with them. She didn't want to pack too much, but also not too little. Since they would drive across the beautiful country, they had to check whether their driver's licenses were valid in South Africa. Also what other papers, except for passports, they needed to have with them. Sarah read through a lot of online forums for tips on what to do and not to do when they drove through the local villages, or in Lesotho, where they wanted to go too. Sarah even visited the South African embassy in The Hague for advice. Chris didn't mind that Sarah took the entire planning of the trip on her. Occasionally he suggested something, which caused his wife to do more research. She enjoyed the planning phase of their trip just as much as he knew they both would enjoy the actual trip.

At last the morning came that the taxi driver rang their front door bell to take them to the airport. It took only a half an hour to drive there and as they unloaded their baggage in front of the terminal building, Sarah spontaneously kissed Chris on his cheek.

"Finally," she said, "it's finally going to happen."

Chris smiled, hugged her and off they went, into the terminal building to find the desk where they had to check in. They were one of the first to book in at desk 11. Only fifteen minutes after they had stepped out of the taxi, they walked through customs and were in the tax-free shopping area of the international airport. Both Chris and Sarah enjoyed browsing the different shops. Just being there already put them in a holiday spirit. In the tax-free bookstore they each bought two books to read on the plane and during their vacation, either by the campfire in the wild parks on in bed in the hotel rooms.

Chris and Sarah installed themselves in a coffee bar not far from the gate where they had to board their flight. They read the back covers of the books the other had bought. Chris had two historical crime thrillers. That didn't surprise Sarah, as Chris had always liked to read about things that happened in history. He preferred real facts to fiction. When Chris read the back cover of the first of Sarah's books, he frowned and looked at her. She anxiously awaited his reaction. He smiled and reached for her other book to read the back cover. This time he didn't frown, but only furrowed his eyebrows. There was a question in his eyes. The books were of an erotic nature, more or less in the same genre as the one she had read months ago. Sarah blushed but said nothing. How could she ever tell him she was interested in trying the things described in the books?

Chris sat with his own thoughts: *Why does Sarah read those books? Does she want to try some of those things? Is she really interested in it or is she only ready the books because her friends do it? Can I even talk to her about it?*

He didn't want to ask her, afraid to embarrass both of them. It had been ages since they talked about their sex life, about their desires and fantasies. Ever since they realized there would be no children, they stopped talking about intimacy; about sex. It was as if the subject was off limits from that moment onward. Maybe during this holiday, he should try to change that. Their marriage was a good one, but something seemed to be missing – a vital part, but not important enough to wreck their marriage. They made love once a week, which was good, but it was more a thing of going through the motions. Something had recently changed in their dynamic. Whether it was the book they both had read or whether it was just a next phase of their lives they were moving into, Chris didn't know. He instinctively felt that if they didn't act on it now, they might still drift apart. That was exactly what they had tried to avoid all these years, after they had to work through the disappointment of not having a family.

From where they sat at the coffee bar they noticed the airline personnel appearing from the doors behind the counter. The stewardesses busied themselves on the computers, talked to each other and looked through some papers. All the while they ignored the waiting passengers.

"Should we move closer?" Sarah asked nervously.

"No," Chris said, "they won't leave without us. The moment the boarding starts, everyone will rush to the gate. We can just as well wait until the main rush is over."

What he predicted indeed happened. One of the flight attendants called all first-class passengers and anyone in a wheelchair or who needed help to get onto the plane. Several people stood up and moved towards the counter. Their passports and boarding passes were checked and they disappeared through the door into the boardwalk that connected the aircraft to the building.

Once this first group of passengers had boarded the plane, the rest of the passengers were called to the counter. Everyone went to the counter at once. Only when about ten people still stood at the counter, Chris and Sarah crossed over to the waiting area and joined the line. By then Sarah's nerves were shattered. Chris stayed calm throughout their wait, but she wanted nothing more than to join the long line. At least then she would have been doing something and it might have calmed her nerves. By the time she stepped through the door of the aircraft and saw the rows and rows of seats inside, her nerves calmed somewhat. Chris and Sarah found their seats and even found space in the overhead compartment directly above their heads to stow their small backpacks. Both kept one book out to read during the flight. As soon as they were buckled in and the wait started for the plane to taxi towards the runway, Sarah's nerves played up again. Her hand crept towards Chris's and she locked her fingers in with his. Chris looked at her in surprise. It had been ages since she last held his hand like this.

Sarah only relaxed once they were up in the air. She couldn't quiet down her nerves entirely though. Sarah had never been in a plane before and credited her nerves to the fact that she would be caught up in this aircraft between all these strangers for so long. She reached for her book and opened it. Losing herself in a story might be what she needed to calm her. Next to her Chris opened his book too. By the time breakfast was served, they were lost in their respective stories.

Chapter Nine
Soraya, Veronica, Madison and Alison

The idea for an overseas trip came up one night when the four friends went out to the theater. Halfway through the play they were bored. They left during the break and went to a nearby bar for a couple of drinks. The more they had to drink, the more they complained about their boring lives. They were the life partners of successful men who preferred their wives to take part in different high society clubs instead of working traditional jobs. The glamour of high society had long worn off. What they did for the clubs was getting more of a drag every day. They had no fun in their lives.

"Let's go to South Africa!" Madison suddenly said.

"Yes!" Soraya and Veronica said in chorus.

The three of them looked at Alison, who was silent a while longer.

"I think it's a good idea," Alison said, and the tone in her voice was enough to bring the other three back to earth.

"But?" Madison asked with a frown wrinkling her forehead.

"We should start with going away for a week," Alison said.

"But whyyy-yyy-yyy," Madison moaned.

"Because we might not be compatible to go on holiday together," Alison said matter-of-fact.

"Why not?" Veronica asked. "We are friends, after all."

"Yes," Alison said, "we are and we spend a lot of time together, but we've never stayed overnight somewhere. Not even for one night. Let's rent a house in a holiday park for a week or ten days. If things go wrong for whatever reason, we go home. If all goes well, we book a trip to South Africa."

The other three women thought about her words.

Soraya was the first to speak: "Alison has a point."

The others nodded. They agreed and with that, it was settled. A month later they were in a house together up in the north of the country. Their husbands had all frowned on this idea, but they never refused their wives anything.

Alison was married to the director of an international laboratory. He started the independent medical laboratory some years ago. Everyone told him it would never be a success because it was too small and with the economic situation in the world as it was, it was a huge gamble to start a new company. He didn't listen but went ahead and within two years he owned one of the best known labs in the country. His company grew. He had to take on more people and move to another building. The company caught the attention of foreign customers. It grew in sales and personnel, and they had to move yet again. At the same time Alison's husband decided that the family should find a house in the upper-class part of town, where he could entertain his international customers in a classy environment. It took a while for the couple to get used to moving around in the social circles of higher society. Their son quickly made new friends at school. Eventually, the parents of those friends invited Alison and her husband to dinner parties. Soon they were part of the 'in-crowd'.

Veronica and her husband were high school sweethearts. Both grew up in the neighborhood where Alison came to live and they never left. Their house was three blocks from the house where Alison and her husband started their high society lives. Veronica's husband worked as a bank manager and his days were much longer than normal office hours. To fill the hours of her day, Veronica volunteered for different charity associations. She had a lot of time on hand as they had no children. Their childlessness was a conscious decision. Veronica didn't want to ruin her perfect figure or her perfect life and her husband didn't care much for children. Veronica was chairwoman of the Christmas association and treasurer of the tennis club. She also worked for two other clubs where she helped to organize different social events. Veronica was always on the run, always busy and barely saw her husband due to his long days. They were still in love and content with the life they had chosen for themselves, but their sex life was almost non-existent.

Madison's husband was a politician. He planned to run for prime minister one day, but to get there he had to work hard. He frequently traveled across the country and slept in different hotels while Madison was at home with their twin daughters. When their girls were still younger, Madison didn't mind being at home without her husband. The young ones kept her busy. However, once the girls grew up and seemed to always be out with friends, Madison was home alone and that bored her. To counter the boredom, she threw herself into the high society club life. She spoke to her husband about finding a job and do something constructive every day, but he refused. He suggested for her to travel with him, but Madison wasn't interested in politics. She figured that if he ever got to be the prime minister, there would be time enough to stand at his side and smile as if she knew everything about politics and what he stood for.

Soraya was born in Brazil. She met her husband when he traveled there for business. He worked for an international construction company and investigated possible projects before they made big investments. Soraya worked as a chambermaid in the hotel where he stayed. They couldn't keep their eyes off each other. By the time he left after one week, he gave her his business card and asked her how he could get in contact with her. The only way to reach her was to call the hotel. He called her once a week and, a month later, he was back. This time the sole purpose of his visit was to court Soraya. He left again after three weeks, only to return again three months later. This time he traveled to Brazil to marry Soraya and take her back home with him. Showered with love by her husband, Soraya quickly adapted to the different culture of the small European country. She had an outgoing personality and liked to connect with other people. Since her husband didn't want her to work, she volunteered her services at different organizations. Not even giving birth to two kids could keep her from her work. She left the kids in the care of a nanny.

The four friends filled the first two days in the holiday house with shopping and swimming. By the third day boredom set in. There were no new shops nearby to discover and frankly, after two days of shopping and buying unnecessary things, they didn't want to go to the shops anymore. The women enjoyed swimming and relaxing, but they were so used to being busy all the time and sitting still for too long bothered to them. On the fourth day, they stayed in the house, not in the mood to go outside because it rained. Halfway through the day they sat in the lounge, sipping tea.

"I'm bored," Alison said out loud what all of them were thinking. "We should find something exciting to do. Something fun. No shopping, though. I've seen enough shops in the last days."

Soraya, who always was the mischievous one, misinterpreted her words on purpose.

"Oh you want excitement? I can give you excitement lady, but I don't think you'll join me," she smiled and winked at Alison.

"What do you mean?" Madison asked.

"Where can we go?" Veronica asked.

"We're not going anywhere," Soraya answered Veronica's question first and then she looked at Madison, "and I mean we can have fun right here. I just doubt whether you will have the *guts* to join me."

"We'll do anything," the three others called out at the same time.

Soraya looked at them, one by one, and smiled.

"Anything?"

The three women all nodded. Soraya stood up, walked to the television and switched it on. Her friends looked at her, puzzled. She disappeared into the bedroom, which she shared with Veronica and came back with her purse in her hand. Soraya sat down and reached for the remote control on the side table. She changed the channels on the television until she found what she was looking for.

"No, serious," Alison said, "the porn channel? Come on!"

"Ha! I thought you would do *anything* for some excitement? See, I told you, you don't have the guts!"

Soraya pointed the remote control toward the television to switch it off again.

"No," Veronica stopped her, "leave it on."

"Yes, leave it," Madison agreed.

"What about you, Alison?" Soraya asked.

Alison nodded. She didn't want to admit to her friends she had frequently watched porn online when her husband worked late and her son was out with his friends. Porn, to her, was something to be ashamed of and not something you watched with your friends.

"Okay, here goes, ladies!" Soraya said after she had used her credit card to pay for a porn movie.

The four women settled in on the two couches. Initially, they experienced different gradations of discomfort, causing them to make silly remarks about the images on the screen. Soon they went quiet and relaxed. Soraya was the first to squirm. Images of a busty blond woman, licking the pussy of a woman sitting on her face and wanking the cocks of the men on either side of her, filled the screen. The pussy of the blond woman was full in view, fingered and fondled by the two men on the screen. From the corner of her eye, Soraya noticed that Alison couldn't sit still either.

"Phew," Madison said and moved in her seat, "I feel a bit flushed."

"Me too," Veronica whispered. Her voice was hoarse with lust.

Afterwards, none of the women could tell how it came as far as it did. Soraya and Alison took their clothes off at the same time. Alison was shy, but once Soraya spread her legs and touched her own sex, Alison did the same. The two other women watched as their friends masturbated and soon they were naked too. Each woman fingered her own pussy, rubbed her own clitoris and fondled her own breasts. Soon, however, they touched each other. Shy and inhibited at first, but they grew bolder. The friends licked, sucked and fingered each other. They kissed, fondled and tasted each other. Some orgasms were quiet ones. Moans and groans guided other orgasms.

By the time the movie ended, the women had no attention for the snowy image that remained on the television. All their shyness had disappeared. They relished in discovering that each of them was different and needed to be touched in another way to reach a climax. None of the women had ever made love to another woman before, but all of them had dreamed about it. At first their movements were exploratory, but soon their actions were all about bringing the other to a climax. None of them preferred one friend to the other. They frequently swapped places. As the day came to an end, they were exhausted, but also fulfilled and relaxed.

They readied themselves to go out for dinner. In the shower, Soraya knelt and covered Veronica's sex with her mouth. She pushed her tongue between her labia, flicking it up and down until she found her erect clitoris. Concentrating on the little button, she sucked it in between her lips and kept on sucking when she slipped a finger into her friend's vagina. Veronica grabbed her own breasts and moaned loud when the orgasm took hold of her body. Madison and Alison showered next. They lathered and washed each other's bodies and 'accidentally' slipped fingers between labia or inside vaginas. Fingering each other hard, they kissed and only stopped kissing when both of them had reached an orgasm. The four women took much longer than normal to get ready to go to town for dinner. On their return from the restaurant, they went straight to bed. No more fucking happened that night, but the rest of their days in the house they returned to caress, lick and finger each other on several occasions.

When they had to check out on the seventh day, none of them wanted to go home. They waited until the last minute to pack their suitcases. In the car on their way back home they were quiet. Alison broke the silence when they were halfway to their destination.

"It's a pity we cannot have the same fun back home."

"Why not?" Soraya asked.

"Well, because… you know. Life. Husbands. Kids. Everything…" Alison said.

"Wait, I have a plan," Veronica said.

"What plan?" Madison asked.

By the time they got home, the plan was clear. They would get together once a week under the pretense that they needed to exchange ideas on how to improve their work for the different charities. Like they suspected, their husbands didn't object, even though their wives would have one more event that would take them out of the house at night. From there on, every Thursday evening, the four women met at Veronica's house. They locked themselves in the basement where Veronica had her office. They put on a porn movie, which they rarely watched. These evenings were all about sex and orgasms. Their games went a step further than in the holiday house. Soraya had sneaked off to a sex shop when she visited another city for her charity work, where she bought vibrators in four different colors. They sat with their legs spread and fucked themselves with the vibrators while watching each other. Sometimes they didn't use the vibrators, but allowed their hands to do all the caressing and touching. They had a huge amount of fun and a countless number of orgasms.

Three months later the women told their husbands about their planned trip to South Africa. They wanted to be based in Cape Town, from where they would go into the townships to do charity work. This time the husbands asked for more information. How long would their wives be abroad? Was it safe to go to South Africa, with the unrest there frequently was in the country? Would they be accompanied by locals when they went into the townships? The wives had answers to all the questions their husbands asked. Those answers satisfied the husbands. Not even the fact that the women would be away from home for three months, bothered the men. As long as the kids were taken care of and the women would be safe, the husbands didn't mind them making the trip.

In the month before their trip, excitement ran high. This caused their Thursday evening gatherings to be more intense. They explored different positions, experimented with anal sex and with pain. Alison discovered that she loved being spanked, while Soraya liked to have her nipples twisted and pinched. Veronica wasn't into pain at all, but loved to fuck herself in the ass with her vibrator, while she frigged her clitoris. Madison discovered a sadistic side of herself. She enjoyed spanking Alison until her ass was bright red, but also feeling the wetness between her own legs when she tortured Soraya's nipples and saw the flashes of pain on her face. Lust and passion for each other mixed with excitement for their trip. It was the drive behind their intense orgasms and exploratory actions.

Alison took care of the arrangements for their trip to South Africa. She contacted different organizations in Cape Town and found a furnished apartment in Sea Point, where they could stay for the three months they planned to be in the country. The plan was that the four women would help with cooking and serving food in two of the townships. They would also visit old age homes to read to the old people or just to keep them company to make their days less lonely. Enough room remained in the schedule for traveling to visit other places in the beautiful country and experience being part of its rainbow nation.

The women traveled to the airport by taxi early one morning, after they had kissed their husbands and children goodbye the night before. At the airport they quickly checked in. They roamed the tax-free shops, where they bought cookies and candy to eat during the long flight.

In the plane, they had no problem to find their seats. They were lucky enough to sit in the first row of their section, in the middle of the plane. The four friends sat together, Madison and Alison on the aisle seats, Soraya and Veronica in the middle. Soraya leaned forward, looked right, then left and whispered when she had the attention of her friends: "Do you have your vibrators with you?"

The other three nodded fiercely, smiled and blushed.

"Of course we do," Madison added to the nodding.

"I found a sex shop online," Soraya said and winked, "it's not far from the apartment. We might just have to go shopping in Cape Town."

The others laughed and they squeezed each other's hands. They were excited about this trip. Even though their lives had been less boring in the past months, they looked forward to being away from home. What excited them even more was the prospect of being together day and night for the next three months and having all the sex they wanted.

Chapter Ten
Kaitlyn

Kaitlyn stowed her cabin luggage in the overhead compartment, found her seat at the window and buckled herself in. She seemed to be oblivious of all the other people around her. Other passengers found their seats, found space for small suitcases and carry-on luggage and buckled themselves in for the takeoff. Someone sat down next to Kaitlyn, but she barely noticed. Kaitlyn's thoughts were with her husband.

Will he still be my husband when I return? Do I still want to be married to him?

She kept on returning to the same questions.

What about the kids? What about my beautiful soul mate? Can I live without him, after the beautiful months we had together? Am I willing... am I able to let him go if I stay with my husband?

She closed her eyes and leaned her head against the cool cabin window.

I don't know. I don't know what I want. What must I do? What's the next step?

Kaitlyn needed clarity and the only way to find it, was to be away from everyone and everything. She wanted no one to influence her train of thought. She had to work this out for herself. Her decision would change the lives of more than only her own. If she stayed with her husband, she would have to let her soul mate go. But, if she continued the relationship with her soul mate, a divorce would undoubtedly follow. She would have to move out and leave her kids with her husband. Was she able to do that? Could she throw away everything they had built up over all these years?

Thankfully, the law firm where Kaitlyn worked as an attorney gave her a month off from work. She had several cases scheduled for the next weeks. Two colleagues took over three of her urgent cases. Trial dates for the other cases Kaitlyn worked on were too far in the future to worry about them. Those could wait until after her return.

Kaitlyn's thoughts traveled back to when she met him – her soul mate. It was totally unintentional. She wasn't looking for anything outside her marriage. Information was all she wanted. Her marriage had come to a point where it was dull and boring and passion seemed to have disappeared out the back door. Making love to her husband wasn't the same as it was before. They were only going through the motions and sometimes more than a month went by without sex. Kaitlyn reached out on social media, trying to find people in a similar situation: married at a young age, still interested in sex and in love but bored with a partner. There were women who answered her, but even though their marriages bored them, they didn't mind the lack of sex as they had a low sex drive. They had no answers to Kaitlyn's questions or any advice to give her, other than that she should accept her life as it was. Kaitlyn didn't want to accept it. She wanted to change things; to bring back the passion into her marriage. She dismissed the advice those women gave her.

One day, *he* answered one of her questions. The more she asked him, the more he intrigued her. He told her about his life. He lived alone, but was involved in relationships with two women. The women knew about each other and sometimes they spent time together. He was in love with both, and they were in love with him.

There's always room for one more.

Kaitlyn stared at these words on her screen, knowing it was a hint towards her. She ignored it and continued to ask questions. Kaitlyn was aware of the existence of polyamorous relationships, but had never talked to someone who claimed to be polyamorous.

Polyamory is not the same as polygamy, was one of the messages he sent her. Another was: *Polyamorous people have more than one loving relationship. It usually, but not always, involved sexual relationships too.*

Kaitlyn was curious to learn more. He shared more about his relationships: *One of the most important things in a polyamorous relationship is open communication between all people involved. It's my task to love them and make them feel special, but also to make sure I spend equal time with each of them.*

Kaitlyn had a million questions, and he answered each one of them. There was something about him that held Kaitlyn's attention.

Can we meet?

Kaitlyn wanted to talk to him face-to-face. She had more questions, but wanted to look into his eyes when he answered them. He seemed sincere in his on-screen messages, but she wanted to see his expression when he told her. They set a date to meet on a terrace in the middle of the city. She was there long before the time they had agreed on. Sitting in the shadow, in the corner of the terrace, she watched every person who walked towards her. He caught her eye the moment he crossed the street. A well-built, confident man in a dark suit and light yellow shirt. No tie. Casual, but smart. Handsome. Kaitlyn's heart beat faster as he approached. She couldn't remember the last time a man had caused her heart to beat like that.

If she hadn't already, Kaitlyn fell hopelessly in love with him that afternoon. He was everything she had ever been looking for in a man. No, that wasn't true. Her husband once was that man. That was when she was still young and immature. This man was the kind of man she needed and wanted for her mature self. Somehow she and her husband had both grown through life, but in different directions. They were not on the same road anymore. Their marriage had become what she had hoped it never would: there was love, but no excitement and no more special moments. Whatever they did, they did with no passion, even when making love. Actually, it didn't deserve to be called 'making love' anymore. They only did what they needed to satisfy their own needs.

It was different with this handsome man. From the moment he took place across from her, sexual tension surrounded them. Kaitlyn had difficulty keeping her eyes off his face. She saw the honesty, love and devotion in his eyes when he spoke about the two ladies in his life.

Does my husband speak about me in the same way? she wondered for a moment. She immediately dismissed the thought and concentrated on the man in front of her. Kaitlyn asked him a million questions, and he answered all of them and elaborated on things she didn't understand. It was hours later that Kaitlyn glanced at her watch.

"I'm so sorry, but I have to leave."

She still had an hour's drive ahead of her and dusk was already setting in. He hugged her tight when he left and whispered in her ear: "There's always room for one more."

Her knees went weak. She gasped. He turned around and walked away. She stared at his back, wondering what he was doing to her. Kaitlyn recognized the sexual excitement, something she hadn't experienced in many years. The next day, they continued their conversation on social media. When he suggested another meeting, she was keen to go.

I'm booking us a hotel room.

She read the words a couple of times before she slowly typed her one-word reply: *Okay.*

His next message was: *It's not only to talk.*

Again she waited before she typed: *I know.*

A week later they both arrived at the hotel at different times. Kaitlyn knocked softly on the door to the room and waited for it to swing open. He held his arms out to her and she walked right into his embrace. They shared the first of many passionate kisses. He hugged her close to him, then held her at arm's length.

"Are you ready for this?" he asked, and Kaitlyn nodded.

"You can still leave and there will be no hard feelings," he talked again, smiling at her.

Kaitlyn was quiet for a moment and then she shook her head.

"I don't want to leave. I need passion in my life," she said.

He scooped her up and carried her to the bed. Their lovemaking was slow and tender, even though their breathing betrayed that they wanted to devour each other. They held back, savoring every moment as they discovered each other's bodies. For the first time in years Kaitlyn felt loved and wanted. For the first time in years, sex excited her. And, for the first time in years, she didn't fake her orgasm.

The first weeks of their affair, Kaitlyn conveniently forgot that she was in fact a married woman. She hid her guilt deep down where it couldn't haunt her. Whenever that tiny voice in her mind told her she was wrong in what she was doing, she went into a discussion with it and justified all her actions. She had several meetings with the handsome man. He was her soul mate. Sometimes they met during daytime, when she took time off from work or stayed out longer for lunch. Other times they met in the evenings and then she told her husband she had to work late to prepare a case for court. Her husband noticed that she was away from home more often than before. He clarified it for himself that the law firm must have taken on more cases than the attorneys could handle.

Kaitlyn became more and more trapped in her situation. Deeply in love with her soul mate, she realized that she still loved her husband. She didn't want to give up her marriage of twenty years just like that, but at the same time, she didn't want to give up the new and exciting relationship with her lover. She was in a place where she didn't want to be and she had gotten herself there. Still in a debate with herself on how to handle this, whether she should tell her husband about her affair or whether to break it off, fate took over. Her husband walked into the kitchen one evening while she cooked dinner. He had an overnight bag in his hand. She instantly recognized it as the bag she had hidden in her car. No words could justify the existence of an overnight bag, let alone explaining the condoms and two vibrators in the bag. The zipper of the bag was open and the expression on her husband's face told her he had already found those items. He knew.

At that moment, Kaitlyn wanted to kick herself for not talking to her husband earlier. This was not the way he should have found out about her infidelity. She should have told him; should have confessed. He didn't even ask her what it was. Her husband saw the answer in her eyes. He threw the bag on the kitchen table, turned and walked out. Kaitlyn heard his footsteps go up the stairs and moments later it came down again. The front door slammed behind him as he left the house. Kaitlyn sat down at the kitchen table, staring at the bag. Her mind was empty. It was only when she smelled something burning that she came into action again. She turned the fire out under all the pans. The kids would be home soon and she had no idea what to tell them. She quickly brought the bag upstairs to avoid any questions. The front door opened while she was still in her bedroom. She heard her kids barging in, laughing and teasing each other. Kaitlyn forced her voice to sound normal, cheerful even, when she called downstairs that their dad wasn't home and they would order pizzas.

The next day, after little sleep that night, she called her husband and was surprised when he answered the phone.

"We need to talk," he said.

They agreed to meet each other in a restaurant in the city. It seemed best to talk on neutral ground. During that talk, Kaitlyn confessed about her soul mate. She admitted that she was in love with the other man, but she also told her husband that she still loved *him*. She tried to explain her confusion. Kaitlyn wanted to come clear with him. She was torn between two worlds and he needed to understand that she still loved him. At that moment, she knew she wouldn't walk out of their marriage without giving them a fair chance to blow new life into their relationship. It broke Kaitlyn's heart to see the hurt in her husband's eyes and knowing she had put it there.

"I thought we were happy," he admitted.

"There's something missing between us," Kaitlyn said, "I miss the passion. It's as if we have lost sight of each other somewhere along the way. I don't even know if we're staying together out of love or habit. We don't long for each other like we used to before. I love you, but I want to stay with you because I *feel* the love between us. I want to have sex with you because I *feel* your desire for me."

Her husband stared at her. It took a while before he spoke.

"But I *do* love you," he said.

"I know you do, and I love you too, but something is missing," Kaitlyn said in a sad voice, "We have drifted apart."

"Do you want a divorce to be with him?"

"No. No," Kaitlyn said, shaking her head. "No, that's *not* what I'm saying. I'm in love with him, yes. He fills a void, but I don't just want to throw away what *we* have."

"Then what *do* you want?" her husband asked, despair obvious in his voice.

"I want us to work on repairing our marriage. I want to get the passion back. But we can't do it ourselves. We need help," Kaitlyn said.

"Help?"

"Relationship therapy. We need someone to guide us through this," Kaitlyn explained.

"Okay. We can do therapy. Will you still see him?"

"No."

That was one of the most difficult things Kaitlyn ever had to do: to contact her soul mate and tell him she was going to fight for her marriage. However, she was not prepared to let go of him entirely. She still wanted him in her life, but she needed a time-out. She asked him to give her three months. After the three months, she would tell him whether she wanted to continue her relationship with him. Kaitlyn needed to fight for her marriage.

"I will wait for you," her soul mate said.

In all earnest and with every good intention in the world, Kaitlyn started the relationship therapy with her husband. The therapist was wonderful and open-minded. Instead of telling them what they should do, she coached them into finding their own way. After some weeks, Kaitlyn briefly touched on the subject of opening their relationship for others. Her husband didn't dismiss the idea, but asked for time to think about it. This earned him praise from the therapist. Kaitlyn fell in love with her husband again. There were butterflies in her stomach. They spent a lot of time together and realized that their marriage was worth saving.

Things were going well, but two things bugged Kaitlyn. First, even though her husband had told the therapist he would think about opening their relationship, he never spoke about it with her. After several sessions he admitted that he didn't want to do it. He was jealous of the man whom Kaitlyn had fallen in love with. He didn't want an open relationship because he didn't want her to be with 'that bastard' again. The other thing that bugged Kaitlyn was that she was still not honest towards her husband. She managed to stay away from her soul mate for only two weeks. She had not seen him since she and her husband started their relationship therapy, but she had contact with him every day. They sent each other text messages. Kaitlyn didn't want to go a day without his words of love. This was unfair to her husband. She knew this, but she seemed unable to stop.

In their next therapy sessions, she tried again to talk to her husband about letting other people into their relationship. The therapist didn't offer her opinion of such an arrangement, but coached them to reach their own conclusions.

"Do you only want to open your relationship so you can allow your soul mate in without feeling guilty towards your husband?" the therapist asked Kaitlyn.

"What are your exact fears to opening the relationship?" she asked Kaitlyn's husband.

"Kaitlyn, how would you feel if your husband falls in love with another woman?"

"Have you never wondered how it would be to make love to a woman other than Kaitlyn?"

They didn't have to answer her questions. The therapist asked the questions and left them to reach their own conclusions. All the questions made her husband doubt himself again, and he asked for more time to consider trying it.

Then disaster struck again. One evening before bedtime, Kaitlyn showered while her husband lay in bed. Her phone rang while she was in the bathroom and it woke her husband, who had dozed off. Thinking it might be an important call, her husband reached over to her phone. It was her soul mate calling. Her husband recognized his name. When Kaitlyn came out of the bathroom, he sat on the side of the bed, his face contorted with anger.

"You're still seeing him, right?" he accused her.

"No, I'm not. I promise, I'm not."

"But you've had contact with him all this time?"

Kaitlyn couldn't lie to him.

"I wanted to break off all contact with him, at least for as long as we're in therapy. I was weak. I don't know how to stay away from him. I have no idea what role he will play in my life, but I cannot think of a life without him in it."

"And what about us then?"

"I want us to be good too," Kaitlyn admitted.

Her husband kept quiet.

"I want you both," Kaitlyn spoke again.

"You'll have to choose," her husband said and with those words he slammed the door on ever opening their relationship and hearts for others.

Kaitlyn was back to where they had started. All the weeks of therapy seemed to have been for nothing and it was because she hadn't been truthful to her husband. She was dishonest with herself and with their therapist. She should have broken off all contact with her soul mate. She and her husband lay together in bed that night but neither of them slept. Kaitlyn was cold and sad all night. In the early hours of the morning she reached a decision: she would go away for a couple of weeks. She needed to get away from both men to decide how she wanted to continue with her life. The next day she told her husband about her decision.

"Where will you go?" he asked.

"To my cousin in South Africa."

He nodded. Kaitlyn grew up with her cousin and if there was one person able to help Kaitlyn see things straight, it was this cousin. Kaitlyn called her work and consulted with her departmental head and the personnel officer. She was granted six weeks of sick leave. She only told them she had a marital crisis, because she didn't want to admit to outsiders that there was more than only that.

A pushback tug moved the plane away from the gate. Kaitlyn glanced sideways and saw that the plane was packed. She had heard that this was common for flights to South Africa. Flying to South Africa the planes were always full, opposed to those flying back to Europe. She returned to her own thoughts.

Will he still want to be my husband if I decide to stay with him? He will have time to think too. Will he ever forgive me? Let alone forgive me, will he ever trust me again? What about my beautiful soul mate? Will he miss me if I end things between us?

A pang of jealousy cut through her heart thinking about the other two women in her lover's life. They had uncomplicated relationships with him. Why could she not? The answer was clear. Those two women weren't married and had chosen never to be. They had the best of both worlds – freedom to do whatever they wanted, a loving relationship and great sex. If she left her husband, he would be alone, but if she left her lover, he would have his two ladies to comfort him.

Will I ever know what I want? Kaitlyn wondered. Her cousin was one of the most rational women she knew and she had always been able to untangle Kaitlyn's thoughts. Two years ago, her cousin married a South African man and moved to his country. Kaitlyn was sad to see her go. This would be the first time she saw her cousin again after she had moved. Would they still have the same bond as they had before her cousin left? Would her cousin still be able to help her? Kaitlyn sighed and shrugged her shoulders. In the next four weeks, things would become clear. She was sure of that.

By then the plane was already in the air and the lights for the seatbelts had been switched off. Kaitlyn had to disturb the other two passengers in her row to go to the lavatory. Back in her seat she took the book she had bought at the tax-free shop, opened it and started reading.

Chapter Eleven
Clearing the crash site

On the evening they arrived, the head of the air crash investigation team – Chief Inspector Victor Reede – called everyone together in the tent they used as an operation center. Captain Clarke and the three police officers from Swakopmund were present too at the briefing. They had been assigned to help.

"In the next weeks, the wreckage will be removed from the crash site and taken to a hanger on the military base in Walvis Bay," Chief Inspector Victor Reede – nicknamed 'Reed' – said, "The goal is to remove the wreckage as soon as possible, but we are doing this according to specific international guidelines."

Reed cleared his throat and looked at the papers in front of him. It was quiet for a long time. Only when feet shuffled on the canvas of the tent floor, he seemed to realize where he was. He looked up, looked at his papers again and continued talking.

"First and most important, the cockpit voice recorder and the flight data recorder have to be retrieved. Since the tail section of the aircraft is still intact, it shouldn't be a problem retrieving either of these devices."

His eyes scanned the faces in front of him.

"You will be divided into two teams. One team will work on either side of the plane. We need photos of every piece of debris. Take photos from different angles, including the surroundings but also close-up photos of the pieces. Tag the piece you've photographed, give it a number and log it on the lists I will provide."

He tapped a stack of papers on the edge of the table where he sat. Once again he scanned the faces in front of him. Eyes as serious as his own looked back at him.

"Once all pieces of the plane are tagged and logged, the army will transport the pieces to the hangar in Walvis Bay."

He was quiet for a while, reading his papers again.

"Before we tag the pieces, personal items of the deceased have to be removed from the crash site. Everything you find – briefcases, handbags, toys, laptops, mobile phones, pieces of clothing, even packages with food or snacks – absolutely everything must be taken to the same hanger in Walvis Bay. Investigators will match personal items to the victims once they have been identified. For as far as is possible…"

His voice trailed off. It was quiet again, but only for about a minute.

"Personal items will be sent to the next of kin."

Everyone present in the tent knew that this part of their job was almost as grim as the part where rescue workers had removed the bodies of the victims. They understood that they might find more victims under the bigger pieces of wreckage. It was unknown whether all victims had been taken to the morgue yet.

"Now," Reed continued, "we are in the desert here and working when the sun is at its highest is irresponsible. No need to get people sick. We start at 6am tomorrow morning and will continue until 11am. Then you can have lunch, sleep, go for a walk, do whatever you want. We start again at 2pm and continue until night falls. I want you to work by daylight, for obvious reasons."

Even though they would work for eight to nine hours every day, the work might go on for weeks. Working according to this schedule, meant that people could concentrate properly on the work at hand, and not be exhausted by the weather conditions before they were done. The briefing ended. Some people went to find something to eat, others went to bed to sleep. The army had set up camp on the Walvis Bay side of the crash site. Military staff supplied this temporary camp with food and drink and maintained the complex communication devices.

Breakfast was served in the military mess tent the next morning, an hour before the work was about to start. At six o'clock the teams were present at the crash site. Chief Inspector Reede was there too.

"Your first priority is to get all personal items of the deceased removed from the site. Please take photos of the debris in relation to the personal items before you remove it. Take all personal items to this side," he waved his arm to the Walvis Bay side of the wreck, "where army personnel will take it over from you and bring it to the trucks. Those trucks will take the personal items to Walvis Bay."

Only the investigators were inside the perimeters of the crash site. They were careful not to disturb anything that might give a clue to the cause of the plane crash. Low-ranked military men and women walked on and off between the crash site and two trucks that waited to take the personal items to the hanger in Walvis Bay. They carried each item with respect. As soon as a truck was fully loaded, it drove off and returned later, empty and ready for the next load. Both trucks left the crash site that morning and returned, ready for the afternoon shift. By eleven o'clock the investigators were sweaty and tired. The sun burned down fiercely. Work stopped for the lunch break. Some investigators chose for an early lunch, others took a nap first and had a late lunch before they returned to the crash site to continue their work.

While the team members took a break, Reed called his superiors in Windhoek. He briefed information through for a press statement to be released that afternoon. The media speculated on the cause of the crash and some of those speculations were horrific. Next of kin needed to know the truth as soon as possible. One speculation was that the plane had been hijacked and forced to fly a different route, and that the Namibian military forces had shot it from the air because it had ignored warnings.

"We cannot confirm or deny a hijacking, but I can confirm that the military has not taken down the plane. It has not been shot down. I repeat: the plane has *not* been shot down. We must wait until the investigators reach a conclusion before we'll know what caused the crash."

It could be months before the investigation was completed.

It was almost a week later before the teams had removed all personal items. They worked in an extremely accurate way. Work stopped at times. Strong men wiped tears from their eyes on finding a teddy bear or a Barbie doll between the rubble. All mobile phones were silent because the batteries had died. It was the same for laptops, tablets and handheld game devices. Investigators found a lot of books – some well used and others brand new and unread. Jewelry, clothes, toiletries and any kind of item that could have belonged to a passenger were taken from the site and transported to the hanger by the trucks. Once all the personal stuff had been removed from inside and outside the plane, Victor Reede ordered for all activity to stop.

"Take the rest of the day off and rest. It's been difficult days and there are more to come. Sleep, walk, go out. Relax. Rest. I'll see you all back tomorrow morning at daybreak."

Most of the team members slept through the afternoon and the night and were ready to start again the next day. Only a handful of the investigators asked soldiers to drive them to Walvis Bay, where they had a couple of drinks and enjoyed adult entertainment. At least for that evening, they wanted to forget about the horrors of the past days or the horrors that awaited them the next.

The next day they started at the beginning again; the same place where they had started when they removed the personal items of the passengers. This time they focused on the wreckage. Again they took photos of everything, and they even shot video footage of the pieces of torn and bent steel that once was an aircraft. They tagged each piece of debris, no matter how small or big it was. Pieces that could be lifted by hand were taken to the side of the crash site, from where army personnel moved it to the waiting trucks. Bigger pieces stayed in place. Once everything was photographed and tagged, bigger equipment would be brought in to lift the wreckage onto flatbed trucks. Those trucks took the pieces of the plane to the hanger at the military base. It took almost two weeks for the teams to complete the documenting process and another week for the bigger pieces to be removed from the site. When all pieces were gone, the teams did another search of the crash site to check for human remains or personal items. They found some.

The members of the air crash investigation team were the first to leave the crash site the next day. The three police officers and Captain Clarke stayed. They helped the soldiers to pack up everything as the military camp was dismantled. The troops readied themselves to return to their base in Walvis Bay. The police force repeated the exercise to close off the coastal road right outside the two towns, Swakopmund and Walvis Bay. This gave the infantry time to remove the detoured road. Infantry soldiers removed the pontoons. Technical military staff cleared away oil and sand from the coastal road. The road was damaged where the plane had crashed and the military repaired this, getting the road ready to be opened again by the end of the day.

The police officers returned to Swakopmund. Military vehicles drove off one by one, taking the soldiers and equipment back to Walvis Bay. By the time the first traffic reached the crash site early that evening, there was no evidence that there had ever been a plane across the road. One man remained: the emergency response team leader. Captain Clarke was the first who arrived at the scene and the last to leave. On the beach, he watched as the sun set into the sea, not quite ready to leave the disaster site.

Chapter Twelve
Candy

Candy was tired of waiting. She had waited to go on this vacation for two months now and now she had to wait to board the plane. Throughout the two months she had noticed how exhausted she was. Always tired. She needed this break. For nine years now she had worked non-stop. It had its downsides to be a highly popular porn star. One downside was to work seven days a week for nine years, without a real break. An upside to the downside was her enormous bank account, which enabled her to organize this luxurious trip. She traveled to South Africa in first class, and in the southern tip of Africa, she would stay in a beauty resort in one of the country's less-known wild parks. A month of pampering, meditation and yoga was what Candy needed to replenish her resources; what she needed to get fit again.

Her thoughts wandered back to the last two months. She played the main role in a porn movie, based on the fairy tale of *Snow White and The Seven Dwarfs*. This wasn't an original idea, because different versions of this fairy tale had been filmed over and over again by several movie directors all over the world. Each of them thought he could do it better than his colleagues. Candy didn't care whether it was an original idea or not. As long as she got laid and paid, she would go along with almost any idea for a porn movie. She liked to play the innocent little Snow White. The seven dwarfs weren't actual dwarfs, but some of the most handsome and muscular male porn stars the director could find. They needed to look like hard workers, and the director had totally succeeded in that. A smile played around her mouth as she remembered…

"And cut!"

Candy sighed when she heard the director's voice. She was on the brink of an orgasm. One dwarf lay under her, his cock buried in her ass and another was on top of her, fucking her pussy. She held one cock in each of her hands, wanking them and two other cocks were on either side of her head. She turned her head from side to side to suck first the one, then the other. The seventh dwarf wasn't in the picture. The plot of movie put him in the kitchen, fixing dinner while the rest of them fucked. They had drawn straws before the fucking started. The seventh dwarf got the shortest straw and had to cook dinner. It was a lame and thin plot, but Candy grabbed every opportunity for good sex.

After the director had stopped them, they retreated to their respective resting and powder areas to have the little make-up they wore touched up. The men had to lose their erections and Candy took a quick shower to clean up for the next take. Candy was convinced that the director enjoyed stopping them in the middle of a hot sex scene. He must be a sadist. Two hours later they returned to the set, ready to do the same scene for the third time. The scene started with the straws and once the seventh dwarf left the set, the others threw Snow White on the bed and tore her clothes from her body. First, two of them got onto the bed next to her and taking turns, pushed their cocks into Candy's mouth. The first one who had an erection moved down between her legs and pushed into her pussy. Another dwarf took his place and Candy worked on it to get his cock hard too. She grabbed two others in her hands and soon lost sight of who was where.

By the time she turned over on her knees and fingers pushed into her ass to prepare her for penetration by a cock, Candy was horny and wanted to be fucked hard. She loved sex and always reached real orgasms on the set. Candy couldn't remember a time she hadn't loved sex. However, over the years she taught herself not to climax too fast, because after an orgasm she lost interest in a scene long before it was a wrap. She learned to hold back as long as possible. That didn't mean that Candy could always contain her horny feelings. Sometimes she needed to be fucked and sometimes she didn't care about the agenda of the movie director. When the urge to climax hit, she just allowed it to happen. Sometimes a scene needed to be done again after she had recovered. Several times she impressed the movie director so much with a scene, that he had the plot changed.

Candy's thoughts briefly returned to the present. She watched an older couple approaching hand in hand.

They smiled at each other. Love radiated from their faces. The couple looked around for a place to sit and eventually ended up across from Candy. She smiled at them and wondered whether she would ever find a love like theirs. Would she ever have that special someone in her life with whom she could share her every thought and feeling? Candy had never been in a serious relationship, not even in her teenage years. She never liked any man enough to want to share her intimate life with him. *What a joke*, she thought and smiled. She fucked many men during her professional life, but she never shared intimacy with any man. Or woman, for that matter. Candy received plenty of attention from men, but up to now, she had not met one that could hold her interest.

It started when she was a teen. The first boy interested in Candy wanted permission from her for only one thing: he wanted to touch her boobs. Candy had developed breasts earlier than the other girls in the class and all the boys – hormones controlled their minds – followed her around. One boy seemed interesting enough. He approached her and Candy agreed to meet him after school. When she learned that she didn't interest him as a person, but his only goal was to touch her breasts, she told him he was a pervert and went home. It didn't stop there. She soon realized that most of the boys were only interested in touching her breasts. In a way it flattered her, but her shy nature prevented her from acting on it.

It took a couple of years before she understood that she held some kind of power over the other gender, and not only because of her well-developed breasts. Candy's body had curves in all the right places. She wasn't thin, but not overweight either. Roundabout her eighteenth year Candy discovered that she loved sex. The first boy she fucked showed interest in both her boobs and her face, which was a relief. He was the same age as Candy and even though they had a lot of fun and sex together, his immaturity irritated her after several weeks. They connected on a physical, but not on an intellectual level. Whenever they went out to a bar or a restaurant, he didn't understand half the things Candy talked about or that interested her. He wanted to party and get drunk and have sex and that was all he could talk about too. They slowly drifted apart and before long everything about him bored Candy, even the sex.

Candy's next relationship was all about sex too. By then she had just turned nineteen. He was twenty-four. She thought that since he was older, they would at least be able to talk about other things than only sex. However, some months into the relationship, when the butterflies disappeared, she realized that she had been wrong. Age said nothing about connecting on other levels than sex. Their sex was good – hot even – but after some time there was nothing else to their relationship but the sex. Again Candy got bored. She told him she had fallen out of love with him and the relationship was over. He asked whether he could at least still fuck her from time to time, but Candy refused. She decided that with her next relationship she would first get to know the man before any sex happened.

After half a year of being single, frustration made it almost impossible for Candy to have coherent thoughts. She needed sex. She masturbated almost daily, but that didn't satisfy her anymore. Candy needed a man's hands on her body, the hard muscles of a man's body against her own soft curves. She wanted a cock inside her. Candy was out of a job at that moment and desperately looking for one to pay the next month's rent. She bought every newspaper in the bookstore and at home she circled adverts for jobs she could apply for. Then she saw the advert in the small classified section. The advert described her: *blond woman with curves and at least C-cup breasts*. Some movie director advertised for a woman with the described appearance to play in a movie. *No acting experience needed*. The heading of the classified section where the advert appeared told Candy what kind of movies this director made.

Candy thought about it for an hour or two and then called the listed number. She received an invitation to a job interview for the next day. Doubting herself, she followed a method her mom had taught her years before: she took a pen and a piece of paper and jotted down the advantages and disadvantages of working in the sex industry. She didn't get far. Under the heading 'advantages' she wrote: *Sex without being in a relationship* and *I will have a job*. There was only one disadvantage she could think of: *I won't be able to tell the family about my job*. She stared at the three points and eventually pushed the paper aside. Candy didn't know what else to put on the list and decided to wait until she had done the interview. She might not even get the job.

She was wrong. Four other women already sat in the waiting room when Candy arrived. The movie director called them into his office for their interviews. After he had spoken to her, the director told her to return to the waiting room. The other women waited there too. Together with the creative director, the movie director joined the women in the waiting room. The conversation seemed casual, but Candy instinctively understood that this was part of the selection procedure. The two directors left the room again. The women were quiet. They didn't have to wait long before the movie director called them back to his office, one by one. Candy was the last to be called. In this final interview she learned that the four other women had left and the job was hers.

The conversation that followed was much more relaxed. So much so that when the movie director asked her to undress because he wanted to see her naked, Candy did it with no hesitation. Even though the job was hers, she had not yet signed a contract and she thought he might still be judging her. The man approached her and walked all around her, looking up and down her body. He stood still in front of her, looked at her breasts and then at her face. She smiled up at him and he took this as permission to touch her breasts. He weighed them in his hands, tried to close his hand around it and squeezed it to confirm that they were real.

"Spread your legs," he said in a hoarse voice. Candy hesitated for a second, shrugged and spread her legs.

The movie director slipped a finger between her labia and discovered the wetness of his new employee.

"I'm going to make you a star," he said in a matter-of-fact voice as he turned around and sat down behind his desk. Candy thought she caught a glimpse of an erection in his pants, but she couldn't be sure as it disappeared behind the desk too quickly.

The man pushed a document towards her. Still naked, Candy walked to his desk. It was her contract – three pages of legal mumbo jumbo. Her eyes searched for the important elements. They offered her a contract for a year and she had to make a minimum of six movies during that year. If she was still in demand by the end of her contract, she would be given a new one.

"Tomorrow I want a list from you of things you don't want to do. Sexual things that is," the movie director said and Candy nodded.

"When you're here tomorrow, I want to take your measurements for different outfits. Not that you will wear any clothes most of the time," he chuckled.

Candy blushed.

"I can give you my list now," she said.

The movie director gave her pen and paper. Her list was short: blood, feces and urine were off limits, as was bestiality. Other than that she listed things she had no experience with, but would like to try, such as anal sex, sex with a woman and sex with two or more men at the same time. The movie director smiled when he read it.

"You'll meet the other porn stars tomorrow," were the last words she heard before she left his office.

Two days after she signed her contract, Candy received her first script. She was to play in a movie about two couples going on a vacation together in a cabin in the woods of Canada. They got snowed in and had to come up with a way to pass the time until the roads opened again. Playing games soon got boring and to spice things up, they changed most of the games into a version of strip poker. One thing led to another and as it did, everyone had sex with everyone. In this first movie, Candy was immediately confronted with two of the things she was inexperienced in: sex with two men and sex with a woman. It made her nervous, but the script looked like fun and she liked the other actors. Since she was the newbie, everyone helped her where they could, even if helping her only meant that they could touch her whenever they wanted.

The movie director gave them one week to work through the script and practice their lines. The beginning of the script had dialogue, but later on it would be more about touching, moaning, licking and fucking. The four actors laughed when they practiced those bits too by dry humping and touching each other the same way they would in the actual movie. Candy learned that this was the way they always did it. By the time they started on shooting the movie, they were comfortable with each other. Even so, the day they started, Candy was nervous. For the first time she would have sex in front of an audience.

Candy soon learned that she worried for nothing. Except that everyone was professional about what they did, no fucking took place on the first day. For the better part of the first two weeks they shot the first part of the movie. In the third week they were mostly naked on the set, but it was not until the fourth week that the first fucking happened. By then Candy was at ease running around naked. Knowing people watched while she fucked, heightened her excitement. She tried her best to make it worth their while to watch her. What she didn't realize at that moment, was that this was the reason she became such a success. Her devotion to her audience was admirable and showed on the camera.

In this first movie Candy tasted a woman's pussy for the first time. The other woman sat on her face as Candy lay with her legs spread and a cock in each hand. One of the male actors had his fingers inside her cunt; the other rubbed her clitoris. A camera was positioned at the bottom of the bed, alternating the focus on Candy's pussy and that of the other woman, who arched her back to make her sex visible to the camera. Candy's tongue pleasured the sweet-tasting pussy hanging above her face. She loved the taste in her mouth and loved feeling the thick and hard cocks in her hands. Never in the past had she thought she would like sucking another woman. Now she had a taste of it, she wanted more.

They took weeks to complete the movie. Candy secretly enjoyed doing the sex scenes over and over again. It helped her to gain more experience, but she also enjoyed the sex. Two months after they had first received the script, the movie was a done.

"It's a wrap," the director called and everyone on the set applauded.

A month after the movie had been released to the public, the movie director informed them it was a hit.

By then Candy was already studying the script for her second movie, but when she learned about the movie's success, there was something else that she needed to do first.

Candy visited her parents and told them about the nature of her work. They knew she had a job, but they didn't know what work she did. Initially her parents were shocked, but after talking some more, they admitted that they weren't that surprised. Candy had always been different than other girls in the family and they should have known she would probably never have regular job. Candy expressed her concern about family members seeing the adult movies with her in it, but her parents didn't worry as much as she did.

"Whoever sees it, would have to admit watching porn," her father said, "and chances are they want to keep it a secret more than you have to worry about them seeing you in a movie."

Once that was out of the way, nothing held Candy back to pursue a proper career in the adult industry. With renewed energy, she studied the script of the second movie, practiced with the other actors and performed for her live audience while the movie was filmed. Her second movie was a hit too and her name became more known in the intimate circles of the local sex industry. The actors always got two weeks off after a movie, to unwind and clear the script from their minds before they received the next script. Some actors stayed away during those two weeks, but Candy used those weeks for research, as she called it. She sat in the library of the company and watched earlier movies to learn from them. She learned about acting, learned about kinky sex, anal sex, gangbangs and more. Sometimes while she watched the movies she masturbated, enjoying the freedom she had at her work. It didn't feel like work to her. She never took a break.

During the two weeks of rest after her second movie, the movie director entered the library while she was watching a movie. Candy paused the movie and waited for him to talk, as it looked like he had something to tell her.

"You've never been fucked in the ass, right?" he said bluntly.

Candy giggled and then shook her head.

"No, I haven't," she admitted.

"Your next script has anal sex in it."

Candy kept quiet.

"Are you up for it?" the movie director asked.

Candy nodded.

"We want to shoot it up close. There will be extra cameras as there's only one first time. We want to see it from all angles. Your ass, the penetration, your face, everything."

Candy nodded again.

"We need to get it right the first time," he continued and Candy nodded again.

He left Candy deep in thought. She had known that this would happen at some time or the other. *Am I ready for it*, she wondered, immediately followed by: *yes, I am*. She had watched quite a lot of movies with anal sex and specifically where the actress got penetrated for the first time, or so it was said. Watching it had helped her some, but what helped her more was searching online for more information. She still had to put the tips she found to practice, and she would do that in this third movie. Two days later she held the script in her hand. The story was simple. She was to play a university student who was still a virgin and seduced by the janitor at her dorm. The janitor was a body builder, and twelve years her senior. He lured her to the gym where he picked her up and put her on top of a pile of tumble mats. Their crotches were at the same height when he stood between her legs.

They started out by kissing and fondling each other. Item by item, the janitor undressed the student. He bent down to kiss and lick her pussy, suck her clitoris and push his tongue between her labia. His tongue moved down to her other hole. Candy was amazed at the warm tingly sensations that ran through her body. Her pussy got wetter than it already was. She forgot about the film crew around her, tuned out all the cameras and focused on the male actor. Only the two of them existed. She followed her instincts, pulled her legs up and spread herself wide for him. The male actor looked at her in surprise, but then shrugged and went along with it. His tongue rimmed her asshole. He pushed the tip inside. She was tight back there. Candy moaned as his tongue pushed in. She remembered that she read somewhere that she should relax her muscles, but with her excitement at the heights it was at that moment, it was almost impossible to relax.

The janitor pulled the student's ass closer to the edge of the tumble mats. With her buttocks halfway over the edge, she was spread nice and wide. He pushed his pants down and freed his erection. It was bigger than average and briefly he wondered whether Candy could take it. He shrugged again, snapped a condom on and poured an extensive amount of lube on Candy's ass. He used his finger to spread the lube around, but didn't penetrate her ass. His cock pressed against Candy's darker opening. Slowly he pushed.

Candy moaned. A mixture of hurt and lust filled her. The male actor's cock opened her up and her first reaction was to tighten the muscles. Then she remembered: *relax!* Candy willed herself to relax her muscles. The tip of his cock slipped in and Candy moaned loud. It hurt, but he was gentle. He kept still and waited for her ass to adjust to the intrusion. As soon as she seemed to relax again, he pushed in deeper and then waited again. Candy felt full and filled. She had experienced nothing similar before. When he pushed further, she kind of pushed back, remembering finding this tip online too. It seemed easier to slip inside her. Pain and pleasure mixed. The male actor pulled back and then pushed in again. His cock went in easier than moments before. Candy looked at him and smiled. Her smile encouraged him to move in and out. He fucked her at a slow pace, but soon Candy spurred him on, asking him to fuck her harder. And harder. The pain combined with the fullness made her pussy ooze. The male actor smiled with surprise when she took the full length of his cock inside her ass. He fucked her harder than the script said he should. Both of them climaxed and he collapsed on top of her.

They were still trying to catch their breaths when the sound of clapping hands reached them. The film crew applauded. Candy blushed a bright red, and even more so when her male counter player stood up and joined the clapping.

"You were brilliant," the movie director said, "simply brilliant! I said I would make you a star, but you get all the credit for that. You were born a fucking star!"

Candy blushed even brighter. She was proud of all the praise, but one thought kept on repeating in her head: *I fucking love anal sex!*

Candy's third movie was her real breakthrough in the adult movie world. Suddenly offers streamed in from all over the world. Everyone wanted to work with her. Candy declined all offers with the same message: *I want to gain more experience before I accept any other offers*. Candy wasn't ready yet to work with someone else. She had only just started in the industry.

She never stopped working for the movie director. Candy started working for him when she was twenty and now, nine years later, she still worked for him. At the end of her first contract, she discussed her next contract with him. He knew about all the offers that Candy had been getting and was thankful that she stayed with him. He offered her a contract which stated that she could make one movie a year with another director if she so wanted. Candy was happy with this clause in her contract and signed. From there on she worked with him for nine months of the year and the other three months she worked with movie directors abroad. Candy never took much time off from work for herself. She always had the two weeks after a movie was done to take time off, but was always busy with her work in some or other way. Gradually over the years she noticed that she needed rest.

The movie director was happy to approve Candy's request for two months off from work. In the years since Candy were onto the payroll, more women came to work for him. None of them became the star that Candy did, but he could continue shooting movies in her absence. Candy told him about her plans to visit South Africa and be pampered in a secluded resort where she hoped no one knew her. He told her to keep her eyes open for possible movie plots. They wrapped up the last movie and before she knew, her bags were packed and Candy was on her way to the international airport.

Only when the couple across from Candy got up she realized she had missed the call for the first-class passengers to board. She quickly dashed to the counter, passing the line, and held her ticket up.

"Sorry, I'm a bit late," she said.

The flight attendant smiled, even though irritation flashed in her eyes when she saw the woman with the huge sunglasses in front of her. *Obviously she's got something to hide*, it flashed through her mind.

Candy boarded the plane and found her seat in the business class. Despite the passengers around her, her seat had enough privacy. She stowed away her cabin luggage, sat down and picked up one of the provided magazines. Candy took off her sunglasses and opened the magazine, totally ignoring her fellow passengers. She was tired and expected to sleep for the better part of this flight, as well as most of the first days at the spa resort.

Chapter Thirteen
Judith

Judith walked up and down the aisles of the tax-free shop and selected packages of cookies and bags of sweets. *I will miss this lovely country,* she thought. She had been here for five weeks and had the most wonderful time visiting different towns and sights. It was well worth saving up for this trip. Judith had set aside money for years and while she did so, she searched for a pen friend in the Netherlands. She found two. Exchanging emails with the one only lasted for two years and then it ended without warning. At first Judith didn't understand why the emails stopped, but then she found the obituary online. Judith continued her correspondence with her other pen friend. Five years into their pen friendship, Judith told her friend she wanted to visit the country. She wanted to stay in a hostel. Her friend, who was a widow just like Judith, put a stop to that. She invited Judith to stay with her and after considering the pros and cons, Judith accepted the offer.

Judith lost her husband after only six years of marriage. They married when they were both twenty years old. Her husband was a kind and friendly man, except when he was drunk. Then he hit her and she frequently called in sick while she was nursing bruises in her face. At first, it didn't happen that much, until they were five years into their marriage. Things got difficult at his work and he found solace in alcohol. Judith had to call in sick more frequent than she did before, because he got more abusive. She considered leaving the marriage after months of battering, when one night the doorbell rang. Judith opened the door and two police officers – a man and a woman – stood in the light of the porch, holding their hats in their hands. She knew what their message was, even before they spoke. Her husband had a fatal car accident. She cried for days. Yes, she was sad, but she cried mostly of relief. Judith vowed never to be married again, and she had kept to it.

She excelled in her work, climbing the secretarial ladder from being one of the typists to being the secretary of the managing director. It was hard work and she didn't always do things by the book. Judith had a healthy sexual appetite and being only twenty-six when her husband died, she was full of sexual feelings and desires. At first, Judith reverted to pleasuring herself. She masturbated almost every day and learned everything about her body. Judith could bring herself to a quick climax to relieve her sexual tension, but also drag her masturbations sessions out over an entire evening before she allowed an orgasm to consume her body. She pleasured herself on and off for two years, but then the longing for a man got too intense. Still, she was afraid to get involved again. Judith had not forgotten the abuse of the man who said he loved her, only to hit her again.

She was still reconsidering her decision not to be married again, when one day a male manager walked into the typists' office. Every woman stopped typing and looked at him where he stood just inside the door. He looked lost, and the typists stared. After several seconds of silence, Judith got up and went to him.

"Can I help you?" she asked.

"I'm looking for the copying room. I thought it was here," he said.

"Oh it's on the next floor," she said.

"My secretary always does it, but she's off sick and I really need copies of this," he said as he nodded his head toward the files he held in his hand.

"Let me help you with those," Judith said and took it from him. She walked out of the room and towards the lifts. He followed her into the lift and to the copy room on the next floor. The typist pool was right below them.

"Won't you get in trouble?" he asked. "I don't want you to run behind on your work."

The typists worked according to daily quotas.

"Don't worry," she said and smiled, "I'm way ahead with my work."

She kept on glancing sideways to the attractive man. Judith noticed the wedding band on the ring finger of his left hand.

"When will your secretary be back?" she asked.

"She's got the flu. She called in sick this morning. I'm afraid she might be away for the rest of the week and it's only Monday."

He sounded desperate. Over the years Judith had witnessed how helpless men seemed to be when they ended up in management positions.

"You know you can have a typist assigned to stand in for your secretary while she's off sick, don't you?" Judith smiled sweetly, waiting for his reaction.

"Will you do it?"

"If you have me assigned, yes I will."

After lunch, Judith moved her things to the manager's office. She was a natural talent and did the work as if she had always been his secretary. Judith answered calls, made appointments for the manager, typed his documents and letters and brought him coffee. The next day, her first full day as his interim secretary, Judith wore a blouse that showed off her cleavage – not too much, but certainly not too little either. The night before, she had an epiphany. She didn't want to be married again, but there were other ways to let men into her life. The man she helped that afternoon excited her. She wanted to seduce him. Yes, he was married, but she could be discreet. Judith didn't mind being the 'other woman'. It would be a perfect fit. She would have a man in her life and he couldn't make any demands, because of his marital status. If he ever came to the idea to divorce his wife so he could be with her, Judith would end the affair. That day, showing off her cleavage, she set her plan to seduce him into action. She had only four days to get him hooked, and she had to be careful. If anyone else got notion of what she was up to, she would be fired.

On her second full day as his secretary, Judith stood right next to him, showing him a letter she had typed. She showed him a specific sentence he dictated earlier and suggested that they formulate it in a different way. He squirmed in his seat with her so close to him. Had she not noticed that he was interested in her, she might not have pursued seducing him. She stood still when his hand crept up her legs and ended just under her bottom.

"Will you have dinner with me tonight?" he asked, his voice hoarse.

"Yes," she said, took the document and walked out of his office controlling each step. Judith did her utter best not to jump in the air with joy that she had succeeded so quickly.

He took her to a restaurant on the top floor of a nearby hotel. They had a beautiful view over the city. He flirted with her, courted her and by the end of the evening Judith had him wound around her little finger. Judith feigned tiredness when he asked if he could come home with her.

"It's better to come over on the weekend. We both have to work tomorrow," she said.

"But I ha…" he stopped talking and nodded.

"Can I at least kiss you?" he asked as they stepped into the lift to ride the fifty-five floors down to ground level.

"Yes," Judith said in soft voice and lowered her eyes to hide the signs of victory showing there, "you may."

Their kiss lasted almost as long as it took to ride the floors down to the exit of the building. He drove her back to the office. Her car was still in the parking lot.

She thanked him for dinner, opened the door and got out. Both drove off to their separate homes.

The next two days, they kissed and touched whenever there was an opportunity and no one could see them.

"Can I come to your place tonight?" he asked her on Friday afternoon. He had his briefcase in his hand, ready to leave for the weekend.

"No," Judith refused.

Disappointment flashed over his face.

"I'm home tomorrow night," she said and smiled at him. Judith wanted him to make an effort for her. Never again would she allow a man to control her. She understood very well it might be difficult for the manager to get away from his wife in the weekend, but if he really had the desire to fuck her, he would make it happen. That was what it all boiled down to after all: fucking. She was tired of pleasuring herself.

He found a way. Less than half an hour after he rang her doorbell on Saturday night, they were naked and fucking on the couch. They never made it to the bedroom that night. He fucked her while she lay on her back on the couch, he fucked her while she lay over the armrests of the couch and he fucked her while she was on her knees on the side table. He came twice that evening and she did about twenty times. Judith was insatiable, but by midnight he had to leave. Judith's first affair with a married man lasted seven months and in those months, Judith made promotion from the typing pool to being his full-time secretary. Their affair ended for two reasons: Judith didn't like that he was getting too controlling about when he wanted to come around to her place, and she found a better prospect than him.

This better prospect was one of her lover's business associates from another company. The associate was higher up the corporate ladder than her lover. Judith always wore skirts that ended about five centimeters above her knees and silk blouses with one extra button undone to show her cleavage. She knew that her female colleagues talked behind her back, but this faded in the light of the men who couldn't keep their eyes off her. They either looked at her cleavage, her legs or her bottom. No one realized it, but Judith knew of every look. When this business associate entered her office for an appointment with her manager, she was instantly intrigued by his appearance. He looked older than her manager. His dark hair was speckled with gray. The suit he wore fitted his athletic body in a way that accentuated his assets – his long legs, broad shoulders and slender built. The moment Judith laid eyes on him, a shiver ran down her spine: she wanted him. Her eyes flashed to his hands. She sighed with relief when she saw the wedding band.

He must have seen her interest or maybe it was her clothes that caught his attention. On exiting the office of her manager, he stopped, put his business card on her desk and said: "Call me."

Judith blushed, smiled at him and nodded. He left her office with a grin on his face. A deep desire burned inside Judith but she waited two weeks before she called him. From the first moment on, she wanted to clarify that she was not to be commanded. He remembered who she was when she explained that he had left his business card with her. She did the same as she did when she started the affair with her first lover. This new man – in her mind she called him 'The Suit' – invited her to dinner that same evening. She accepted the invitation. He saw it as a sign that he would fuck her the same night, but Judith held it off for more than a week before she allowed him to visit her at home on a Friday night. By then she had him eating out of the palm of her hand.

'The Suit' was not only a better lover than her manager, but he also arranged a promotion for Judith. He played golf with a senior manager and convinced him he should have a different secretary. He told his golf partner that his current secretary was rude and unprofessional and praised the wonderful and professional way that Judith interacted with him when he visited her boss. Judith acted surprised when she heard about her promotion from secretary of a junior manager to that of a senior manager. 'The Suit' was in her life for several months, until he had served his purpose.

More men followed. Judith slowly climbed the corporate ladder. Sometimes she fucked the men with ulterior motives and sometimes she fucked them because she really liked them. All the time, she was in control. Not once did Judith allow any man to decide the pace of their affair, or to boss her around. The moment a man tended to be too dominant, too demanding, she kicked him out, no matter how much she liked him. She never worried that the men would be nasty to her or try to ruin her career when she ended an affair. They had a lot more to lose, because they were all married and besides their marriages, their careers were on the line too.

Judith earned a secretary's salary, and even though she moved higher up the corporate ladder, her salary wasn't large. However, the men loved giving her presents and many times they gave her money. They paid for holidays, but those holidays were always in the country. Judith didn't mind this, as she could save up her own money for the overseas trip she longed to make. She had once traced the bloodline of her ancestors back to the Netherlands and since then she had a deep desire to visit the country. That was what she saved for, to visit the small, intriguing country she had read so much about. Judith wanted to travel to the Netherlands while she was still vital and in good health. She had it all planned out.

Then the unexpected happened: she fell in love.

She met Hank in a bar one night around Christmas. Judith barely went out by herself, but that one night, on her way home, she hopped into a bar for a drink. She wasn't in the mood to be home all alone and her current married lover would not be with her until after Christmas. That was the only thing that still got to her: not being able to spend the holidays with a special person. Hank sat at the bar when she walked in and took place on a stool close to him. She ordered a Chardonnay and halfway through her first glass they started a conversation. Hank wasn't an attractive man, but he had immaculate manners. It was obvious that he took good care of himself. *Or his wife does,* Judith thought. The wedding band on his ring finger didn't go unnoticed. According to her own set of rules, it was safe to talk to him.

Afterwards, she wasn't able to tell what made her deviate from her normal routine. Maybe another year of loneliness during the holidays had finally gotten to her. Hank went home with her and they ended up together in her bed. Later, it was as difficult for her to let him go as it was for him to leave her. He visited her on the day after Christmas. None of her other lovers ever did this. On New Year's Eve he paid her a quick visit early in the evening to give her a kiss and a hug. Every day, all day long, Judith only thought of Hank. He was in her mind constantly. When her lover at that time asked to visit her early in the New Year, she made up an excuse why she couldn't see him. It didn't take Judith long to realize that she was in love with Hank. Suddenly, all her well-guarded rules disappeared. Hank set the pace in their relationship and for the first time since her husband died, she didn't mind. Hank made time to see her and take her out, but they always went to places where he knew his wife or their friends wouldn't see them. Sometimes they drove for an hour to go out for dinner. But, Judith didn't mind. She was in love and she loved every minute she spent with him.

Judith was thirty-nine when their affair started. She had several lovers in the years after her husband died and she enjoyed all of those, but she never fell in love with any of them. It was different with Hank. She fell hard for him. He never stopped being a gentleman when he was with her. Not once did she feel threatened by him, even when he sounded upset with her. Because yes, just like a regular couple they had heated discussions, but he never lifted his hands or raised his voice. They sneaked off on a holiday together, when his wife went off to Europe with a group of her friends. His kids were grown and had left their parental home. Hank booked them a holiday in a neighboring country where they went hunting and camping. Judith loved being with him day after day. She couldn't imagine a life without Hank in it.

When Hank's wife fell ill seventeen years into their relationship, Judith stood by him. Judith was fifty-six. She saw him less than she did before, but he still came to her place whenever he could get away. His wife was sick for two years before she died. In the weeks just before her death, Judith almost never saw Hank. She was there for him when he called her, when he cried about losing his wife, about the grief of his children for losing their mother. She supported as best as the situation allowed her. Judith didn't attend the funeral, but she waited at home and Hank came to her right after it. She allowed him his grief, his sadness and comforted him. For months. A year. He didn't come to her as frequently as he did before his wife died. Judith thought it was because he was still grieving.

Then the blow came.

Judith tried to call Hank after she had not heard from him for more than a week. This was unlike him, not to keep in contact with her. There was another week of worries and panic before she found out that Hank was married. Married! To his secretary! A woman twenty years her junior and twenty-three years younger than Hank. Judith was devastated. She had no idea what to do. How did this happen? The blow was too hard for her to think straight. She called in sick the next day, for the first time in twenty-five years. Her boss instantly knew that it was serious, and it was. Judith had a nervous breakdown. She was home for months before she returned to work again. However, Judith was not as efficient anymore as she was before. She seemed to have lost her touch and she hated it. She hated that she had turned into an old woman. She hated her work and she hated her colleagues. Judith detested the smug men in their designer suits. She hated the rat race to get to the top. Everything appalled her. After so many years of faithful service, her manager arranged for Judith to go on early retirement. Judith was thankful. She didn't have the stamina to start over. She was done with work, and she was done with men. For good.

It took another year for Judith to see the beauty of life again. She came across her notes of her ancestors when she cleaned up her computer room and that was when she searched for pen friends. Five years later, she had saved up enough money from her earlier savings, her pension and the lump sum she had received from her former employer. Judith blessed the day she stepped off the plane in the Netherlands and started the biggest adventure of her life. Her pen friend waited for her when she arrived at the airport. This friend lived in the city center of Utrecht, which suited Judith just fine as she could travel anywhere in the country from there. And, she did. She traveled all over the place. Each morning she got up before daybreak and she was on the first train out of the station. She traveled to the north, to the south, to the east and to the west. Sometimes her pen friend joined her, but since she was not all too healthy anymore, Judith mostly traveled alone. Judith preferred being alone. She had her meals while she traveled, not wanting to burden her friend to cook for her.

By the time the five weeks were over, Judith had ticked off everything on the list of things she wanted to see. She saw more places than she had planned to see before she left South Africa. Not one day went by without her visiting a new place. The five weeks flew by. When she packed her bag for her flight home, Judith felt sad but also healed. She hadn't thought about Hank since she stepped off the plane and there, packing for her return trip, she realized that her heart had healed. Judith first packed the souvenirs from the different places she had visited. They were in plastic bags with notes inside to remind her of all she had done and seen. On the pieces of paper, she had even jotted down what her mood was on the day. Judith planned to make several scrapbooks back home, combining her photos and the different souvenirs, such as napkins, maps, business cards and promotional matchbooks.

Early the next morning, even earlier than on her days traveling the country, Judith left the house. She hugged her friend tight.

"I wish I could come back next year," Judith said, but she had used all her savings and would probably die of old age before she could make the trip again. She was already halfway through her sixties. They promised to write each other soon. Judith wiped away a tear as she waved at her friend when the cab pulled away from the curb. On arrival at the departures hall, Judith rushed to get a trolley for her suitcases and paid the taxi driver. Before long, she had checked in, cleared customs and was roaming the tax-free shops.

At the gate, she waited until the economic class passengers were finally called to board. Now that she was about to get on the plane, Judith was excited to be back home. She had fun visiting this unique little country and learning more about its culture, but her heart was down in the south of Africa. With that she didn't think of Hank, but her own home, her own place, her own stuff. She would go back to her house and relive this trip over and over again while she kept up corresponding with her pen friend. Judith was full of plans to rekindle friendships in her home country. Not with the men whom she had affairs with, but with her female friends who she had neglected in the past years, for her own selfish reasons.

Judith settled into her seat with a content smile on her face. She checked the watch on her arm and estimated that she would be home just before midnight. She looked forward to sleep in her own bed again. Judith reached for the crosswords book and pencil she had bought in the tax-free shop, and started on the first crossword puzzle.

Chapter Fourteen
Kim and Lora

Kim and Lora grew up in the most southern tip of Africa. Their parents lived in the same neighborhood, only two streets apart. The girls went to different primary schools, but ended up in the same class in the first year of high school. Both were shy and didn't fit in with the popular crowd. During breaks they sat alone, reading and eating their sandwiches until the bell rang and class started again. It took half of that first school year for them to talk to each other. Once they did, they spent every break together, still reading and eating their sandwiches but not alone anymore. During class they always chose desks next to each other. They became best friends and inseparable.

After school, Kim and Lora worked on their homework and studied for tests together. In their first two years of high school their parents didn't allow them to sleep over. It changed in the third year. Because their grades were excellent, their parents agreed to two sleepovers every month. It was limited to two nights to make sure the girls still studied hard and kept up their good grades. Kim and Lora preferred to have their sleepovers on Friday nights. This meant that they could go to the other's house straight from school, where they spent the afternoon and the next day together. On Sundays they had to be up early to go to church with their own parents.

Both girls had a conservative upbringing. Their fathers worked and their mothers stayed at home to tend to the house and raise the children. This was almost unheard off in the modern times, but both their fathers were old-fashioned and didn't want their wives to work. Kim and Lora each had a brother. Kim's brother was three years younger than her and Lora's brother was four years older. By the time the girls started with the sleepovers, Lora's brother had left for university. Most sleepovers happened at Lora's parent's house. There they didn't have to deal with Kim's younger brother, who constantly wanted them to entertain him or teased them all evening by knocking on the door or throwing pebbles from the garden against the bedroom window.

Neither Kim nor Lora was interested in boys. Halfway through their third year in high school, almost every girl in their class had a boyfriend or was in love with a boy whom they hoped would become a boyfriend. Kim and Lora weren't interested. They didn't even notice the boys looking at them. They were only interested in their friendship, their schoolwork and their books. They always had enough to talk about, whether it was discussing something from their history class, solving a mathematics problem or talking about a book they had read. Their parents were grateful that their daughters weren't interested in boys yet, because they didn't have to worry that the girls would do something irresponsible.

One Friday night, just into their fourth year in high school, they lay together in Lora's bed, the same way they had done many times before during a sleepover. Afterwards, neither of them could say how it happened. Lora lay on her back and Kim on her stomach. The faced each other while they talked about different subjects, laughing and enjoying their time together. In a moment of silence, as if pulled together by a magnet, their lips touched. Soft at first, then harder. Their tongues explored the other's lips and tongue. Their kiss gained passion and was as natural to them as when they talked about books. There was no shyness between them. It was that night, when Kim slowly moved her hand over the curve of Lora's breasts, over her flat stomach to her waiting sex, that they realized for the first time they were in love.

Their actions were perfectly natural. Neither of them had ever made love to anyone before, but their instincts told them what to do. Kim cupped Lora's pussy through her panties. The fabric was damp with her excitement. Lora moaned into Kim's mouth, as they kissed and she felt the firm touch between her legs. She struggled to reach for Kim's breast, craving to touch her body, but Kim pushed her away.

"Not yet," she whispered. She smiled at Lora, moved her hand up and slipped it under the Lora's top. Erect nipples awaited her fingers. Lora and Kim looked into each other's eyes as Kim pushed up Lora's top. She covered Lora's breast with her hand and squeezed lightly, causing Lora to arch her back and push her breast hard against Kim's hand.

Passion was their guide. Kim's mouth covered a nipple while her hand found a way inside Lora's panties and gently stroked the puffy labia. Running her finger along her friend's slit, she reached the wetness between the lips. She dipped her finger in it and spread it up and down Lora's intimate folds. Kim felt the hard button at the top of the slit and rubbed up and down over it, in a gentle pace. This made Lora moan louder. She grabbed a pillow and held it in front of her face to muffle her moaning sounds. Kim, who enjoyed giving her lover this much pleasure, moved her finger down, slipped it inside Lora and brought it back up to Lora's clitoris. She pressed down harder. Lora breathed in hard and wriggled beneath her.

"Shall I fuck you with my fingers?" Kim whispered, surprising herself with her choice of words.

In one swift movement Lora removed the pillow in front of her face and nodded fiercely.

"Yes, please. Please do it!"

Kim didn't need more encouragement. She moved two fingers between Lora's labia and found the entrance. There was a barrier when she pushed her fingers in. She pulled back and pushed back in again, but with more force than the first time. Again she met the same resistance.

"Just do it," Lora whispered.

Again Kim's fingers disappeared inside Lora. She felt the barrier but pushed on. Lora let out a short shriek and then a deep sigh. The obstacle was gone.

Kim watched Lora's face as she fucked her friend with her fingers. Lora's eyes were closed, her mouth half open. Her tongue touched her lips. She closed her mouth; opened it again. Her breathing came in short puffs until she let out a long low groan as her pussy muscles gripped Kim's fingers. Lora experienced her first orgasm.

Kim rested her head on Lora's shoulder.
"That was beautiful," she said, "to watch you climax."
"I want you to experience it too," Lora said as she turned on her side and pushed Kim onto her back.
Lora, however, had something else in mind. She moved down to the edge of the bed and bent over to pull down Kim's panties. The girly fuzz between Kim's legs was as dark as her hair. Lora pushed Kim's legs apart and watched as the bright inner pink of her pussy appeared. Kim was wet. Moisture glistened on and between her labia. Lora lowered her face to her friend's crotch. Kim watched in awe as Lora planted a kiss on her pubic hair and then pushed her tongue between her labia.
"Mmmmm," Lora said, "I like…" she licked again, "the taste…" and licked again, "of this."

Kim blushed a little, but spread her legs wider when her friend bent her head back down to the waiting wetness. Lora went with her instincts, moving her tongue up and down Kim's slit and pushing in her tongue as far as she could. She repeatedly returned to Kim's clitoris, which she licked and sucked and sometimes even softly trapped between her teeth.

Irregular movements of Kim's body announced that she was close to an orgasm. Just like Kim did with her, Lora pushed two fingers into her friend's vagina. Her actions were firmer than those of Kim earlier and even though she felt the obstacle, she pushed right through it. A sharp intake of breath came from Kim, but Lora didn't stop finger-fucking her friend, or licking her. Kim inhaled deeply and held her breath. Her body stiffened and only when the orgasmic spasms of her body subsided, she exhaled again.

Lora crawled over the bed and lay down next to Kim.
"Look what I have done," she said with pride in her voice.
Kim opened her eyes and saw the two fingers Lora held in front of her eyes. Her eyes grew wide at first, but then she smiled. She lifted her hand to look at her own fingers. A mixture of pride and embarrassment made them giggle. Both talked at the same time.
"It's blood!" they said in choir.
They had just given each other their virginity.

That night they made love again. Now that the last puzzle piece had fallen into place, they couldn't get enough. They explored every bit of each other's bodies. Lora locked her bedroom door for the first time that night. The two young women – they could hardly be called girls anymore – slept naked in each other's arms. When they woke the next morning, there was no shyness, guilt or regret about what had happened the previous night. At the breakfast table they were as happy and friendly as always. Lora's parents didn't notice the change in the girls, but Kim and Lora did. They had both found an inner peace.

Their cloud of love and happiness disappeared beneath their feet some weeks later. It had suddenly dawned on them they had no idea how to tell their parents about their lesbian love. To Kim and Lora, it was clear – they wanted to build a life together. The conservative community, their old-fashioned parents and their instinctive understanding that they would be separated if they said anything about their love for each other, had them in despair for weeks. They talked about it a lot – at school during the breaks, after school on their way home and in the weekends when they were together. Kim nor Lora talked to anyone else about their dilemma. Whenever someone came too close, they stopped their whispering. They still studied hard, but they kept on returning to the same discussion: their relationship. Because yes, in the meantime, their friendship had deepened to a full-blown loving relationship.

After weeks of discussing it, they reached the decision that it would be better to keep their relationship a secret, at least for as long as they lived at home. When they finished high school in less than two years, they would both enroll at the same university as far away from home as possible. A new environment would give them the freedom to come out as a couple. Their parents suspected nothing. When the time came, they enrolled at the same university. It seemed only natural for their parents to suggest that the two girls share a student room to minimize their living costs. Kim and Lora were ecstatic when they learned that they didn't have to live in a dorm. Their parents found them a small one bedroom flat just off-campus. They explained to Kim and Lora that they had to share a room. With serious faces Kim and Lora said that they understood, while inside they were ecstatic that they could live together as a couple.

Kim and Lora thoroughly enjoyed their student years. They didn't follow the same course, but they still studied together and went out to parties together. They were inseparable. Both found a job at the same supermarket where they worked as often as their studies allowed. Kim and Lora shared a bed and made love whenever they desired. After all the time they had been together, they still couldn't get enough of each other. They were friendly with other students, but just like in high school they were never part of a bigger group of friends. Men showed their interest and always got a friendly answer or a smile, but the young women showed no mutual interest. Kim and Lora were content with each other and after years of being a couple, they knew they belonged together. During holidays they visited their parents and never once spoke a word about their relationship. They were careful not to let anyone see the true nature of their friendship. In all the years together, they still hadn't found a way to tell their parents. They didn't know if they ever would.

In their last year at university they realized that they had to talk to their parents. Soon they would have their degrees, find jobs and follow their plans to build a life together. They both regretted that they had kept their parents uninformed for so long. However, in the meantime there had been more tolerance in the country for same-sex couples, and they wanted their parents to accept this too. Their parents still had conservative views, but Kim and Lora were convinced that they would eventually accept the love of the two women.

"Parents want their kids to be happy, right?" Kim said to Lora, who agreed.

No matter how much they wanted to inform their parents, they didn't know how and when to do it.

"Let's go to Amsterdam when we have our degrees," Lora said one day while they were studying.

"Will we find jobs there?" Kim asked with a confused expression covering her face.

"No, silly," Lora laughed, "I mean let's go there for a holiday. We deserve a holiday, don't you think? We've been studying hard for years! Maybe when we're away from all this and in a country where same-sex relationships are fully accepted, we will finally think of a way to tell our parents."

Kim was quiet for a while, mulling Lora's words over in her mind. She looked at her girlfriend and a smile slowly formed around her mouth.

"Yes," she said, nodding and laughing, "yes! Yes, let's do it!"

Their parents were agreeable when they told them about their plan to visit Amsterdam. Secretly, they hoped the girls would continue studying when they returned from their trip. The economic situation in the country was bad and work opportunities were scarce. Plans were made; tickets and a hotel booked. Kim and Lora planned and paid for different excursions they wanted to go on during their holiday. Their parents gifted them each an amount of money, which, together with the money they had saved, gave them enough to visit Amsterdam for five weeks. Their final weeks at university were spent studying with a constant undertone of excitement for their upcoming trip. Their enthusiasm for the trip translated into sexual excitement. They made love even more than they did before.

A Sunday afternoon found them naked on bed. Lora had her hand behind her head as she looked at the ceiling and talked about the places they were about to visit while in the Netherlands. Kim was on her side next to her, pushed up on her elbow, her head resting on her hand. With her free hand she trailed lines up and down Lora's naked body. Goosebumps appeared and Lora's nipples stiffened. While Lora talked, loud murmurs of assent escaped her mouth while her tongue flicked over the erect piece of flesh. Lora ran her nails up and down Kim's back – not hard, but not entirely soft either. Kim swung a leg over Lora's and rubbed her sex against her lover's leg. She was wet and all ready for her next orgasm. Lora stopped talking. Their movements grew more urgent. They kissed, they sucked and they licked. They moaned, the sighed and they breathed hard. Soon they sat across from each other, their legs intertwined and their pussies touching as they rubbed them against each other.

Both of them had their pubic hair shaved with only a thin strip of hair left above the slit. The dark hair of Kim contrasted nicely against the blond line of hair between Lora's legs. They had always been an attractive pair to see together – one with dark hair and the other blond. But at that moment neither of them cared about whether they were attractive or not. Their lust needed to be quenched. Kim reached over to the side table and opened the drawer. In their university years they had bought several sex toys. One of those was a double dildo, their favorite toy and the toy Kim reached for now. She grabbed the lube from the bedside table and let a couple of drops fall on either end of the dildo. One end disappeared in Lora's cunt, before she inserted the other end between her own legs. The women moved their hips, fucking each other with the dildo. They started at a slow pace that gradually quickened. They both lay on their backs and bucked their hips in an uncontrolled tempo until their orgasms stopped all movement.

Three weeks later they finally boarded the plane to Amsterdam. For five weeks they didn't have to worry about study or work or their parents finding out about their intimate relationship. On arrival in Amsterdam and while waiting for their suitcases to appear on the baggage carousel, Lora slipped her hand into Kim's. They smiled at each other and stood hand in hand until they had their suitcases. A shuttle brought them to their hotel, where they checked into their room. The first hour passed with them organizing their clothes into the closet and drawers and their toiletries in the bathroom. They looked longingly at the bed, feeling frisky and excited, but since it was almost time for lunch, they went out and explored the neighborhood. In the lift they slipped their hands into each other's again. Kim and Lora walked through the hotel lobby and out onto the street, for the first time ever showing the outside world they were lovers. No one looked at them with obvious disapproval, something that both women noticed with relief. During lunch, they kissed and hugged and still they got no strange looks from anyone around them.

They spent most of the afternoon out on the streets of Amsterdam, getting to know the neighborhood around the hotel. Lora and Kim enjoyed the freedom to express their love in public. Not only that day, but every day of their trip. They traveled to Germany, Belgium and France by train and it was the same everywhere. No strange looks from anyone. No nasty remarks. No insensitive questions. In the last week of their holiday, they sat in their favorite spot in a small cafe just down the street from the hotel.

"This is how it should be," Kim said and Lora looked at her.

"We should not be ashamed of our love. We should never be ashamed to show the world we love each other," Kim continued.

"I never want to go back to how it was. I don't want to hide my love for you. Never again!" Lora agreed.

That night, as they lay with their arms around each other, they finally admitted that there was no easy way to tell their parents. There was only one way to do it: once they were back home, each of them would tell their own parents. They believed that their parents would need time to accept the situation as it is, but they would accept it in the end. While they adjusted to the idea, Kim and Lora would search for a house.

Both had job offers before they left for their holiday. Their new jobs started three weeks after their return to South Africa and they wanted to be settled in their new house before they started their jobs.

In the last couple of days before they had to board the plane back home, they didn't speak about the upcoming conversations with their parents. They visited more museums and said their goodbyes to friends they had made during the five weeks. On their last night in Amsterdam, the owners of their favorite cafe surprised them with a farewell party. Kim and Lora cried, sad that they had to leave all these wonderful people behind, but thankful that they had met them. There were promises of keeping in contact and visiting each other. It was late when Kim and Lora returned to their hotel room.

They snuggled close together in bed, all worked up after the wonderful evening. Their lovemaking was that of two lovers who had known each other long enough to know everything about the other's body. Kim and Lora took their time, as if their slow actions could make the time go slower. Sated after several orgasms they lay together, staring at the ceiling when the front desk called them. It was time to get up. The shuttle to the airport arrived half an hour later.

Less than two hours later they found themselves between the tax-free shops of the international airport. There was still over two hours before their flight would depart. Kim and Lora roamed the stores to find last-minute souvenirs for the people back home, and they bought snacks for the long flight. Afterwards, they casually strolled towards the gate where their plane waited. It had become habit for them to walk hand in hand and this time was no different. Close to the gate they sat at a coffee bar, where they ate breakfast. They fell silent now and then, both thinking of the talks they were about to have with their parents the following day. Or, maybe even that evening, depending on how tired they were after the flight.

Before boarding started, Kim and Lora went to the ladies' restroom. On their way in a couple dashed past them. The man pulled the woman behind him and they were obviously in a hurry. The female couple heard the woman laugh. They smiled and winked at each other when they saw the couple in the line later, ready to board the same plane as them. The passports and boarding passes of Kim and Lora were checked. They entered the jet bridge towards the plane, stopped halfway and with tears in their eyes they looked back from where they had come. The five weeks in Amsterdam had shown them the life they wanted – the freedom to be who they were. But, they had to return to their own country, where they would build their life in a community that still had more to learn about accepting same-sex couples.

Chapter Fifteen
The last minutes

"Now I will never get to meet him," Cathy in seat 37A whispered.

There was panic all around her. People screamed and cried. Some prayed. Others were silent. Chaos reigned around her while the plane headed down in a steep angle. She knew she would die and never meet him, her 'Mr. Right'. Only a miracle could save them, and that miracle wasn't going to happen today. Cathy closed her eyes and called the image of his face to her mind – the face she had seen on her laptop screen so many times in the past months; the face of the man she fell in love with even though she had never met him in real life.

"I love you. I love you. I love you," she repeated over and over, as if he could hear her.

The impact of the crash cleared all thoughts from her mind and all words from her mouth.
Forever.

Anthony sat next to Cathy. Chaos was all around them, but the woman next to him was calm. Her lips moved, but he didn't hear her words. Somehow her calm demeanor worked through to him. He felt the panic inside, but he didn't show it. Just like Cathy, he understood that death was inevitable. He could spend his last moments panicking, but he preferred to spend his last moments with thoughts of his wife and children. His wife! Anthony reached for his mobile phone. It surprised him that there was a signal when he switched it on. He scrolled to his wife's name, tapped on it and typed: *Plane is going down. I love you fore...*

He never finished the text.

In the back of the plane Sylvia clung to Brian's arm.

"Brian, we're not going to die, are we? Please Brian, tell me I won't die?"

"No my love," Brian said, holding Sylvia close to his chest, happy that she didn't see her fear reflected in his own eyes, "we won't die. The pilot will have the plane under control in no time."

Sylvia sobbed softly, her face buried in his chest. Brian looked out the window and saw how the clouds flashed by as the plane dove to the earth at a terrible speed. He closed his eyes, not wanting to see his death coming closer. He didn't believe his own words, but he wanted Sylvia to be calm. He wanted her to be comfortable and content in her last seconds. Against his chest, panic raced through Sylvia's body. Even though he lied to her, Sylvia believed him. She held onto him. He was the last one she wanted to feel against her, the last living person whose arms she would ever feel around her.

"I love you, Brian," she said.

"I lo...."

Brian never finished his last sentence.

In their seats somewhere in the middle of the plane Kim and Lora hung forward in their seats. They looked at each other, each with an arm around the other.

"I love you," Kim said to Lora.

"I love you too," Lora replied.

There was so much more they wanted to say. In the past five weeks they had seen how beautiful their life could be when they live together as a couple. They were happy and the world should know about their love. They didn't want to die, but they understood without fail the end was near. They would not survive the crash. They had a life ahead of them and it was about to be taken from them. Their parents would never understand how special they were to each other.

Sarah grabbed Chris's hand when they realized that something was wrong with the aircraft. They looked around them, hopeful that one of the staff would tell them that the problem would be fixed soon. No one came. With their heads between their knees, their fingers still locked together, they kept their eyes on each other, but neither spoke. It has been so long since they talked about their deepest feelings, that even this close to their death, the words eluded them. Even the simple words *'I love you'* didn't cross their lips. A deep understanding filled them both: *we were happy, happy in our own way. Despite all the blows that life dealt us, we were happy. No one can take that away from us.*

Chris tightened his grip on Sarah's hand and a slight smile formed around her mouth. That was the last thing Chris saw.

Kaitlyn listened to the screaming and crying around her. Panic formed a ball in her throat, but no sound came from her mouth. *Why is this happening? How could fate be so cruel? He will have two women to comfort him, but who would comfort my husband? What about our children? They don't know about my infidelity, but will he keep it from them forever? Will they have to go through life knowing their mother cheated on their father? Will my husband be okay without me? Will he always love me? Will he ever know just how much I love him?*

In the moments before the crash, Kaitlyn had no more doubts about what she wanted: to fight for her marriage. She cried softly. Her husband would never know how much she loved him. He would never know that she wanted him, and not her soul mate. It took death to bring her clarity. Tears dried on her cheeks long after the aircraft impacted with the ground.

The moment it was clear that something was seriously wrong with the plane, Joe and Mattie realized that their happiness was more short-lived than they had expected it to be. With their eyes on each other, the knowledge dawned on them that they had to say goodbye far sooner than either of them had ever imagined. Sadness filled both of them, but mostly there was acceptance. They were grateful for the wonderful time they were together. They had the privilege of loving and being loved again. Joe pulled Mattie closer and kissed her before he whispered in her ear: "I will love you forever."

There was no time for Mattie to respond.

Judith woke up with a start when the crosswords book slipped from her lap. She had fallen asleep. She reached for the book and only then realized that something was wrong with the plane. People around her cried and screamed in panic. It took a couple of seconds more for her to shake the sleep and understand that the plane was going down. Going down hard. Judith, who grew up in a religious family, but in her adult life never went to a church, reverted to her upbringing in this hour of death. She prayed and was still praying when the plane hit the ground.

In the business class section one woman was oblivious of what happened around her. Candy had a blindfold in front of her eyes and ear plugs in her ears. She took a sleeping tablet half an hour into the flight and the flight attendant had let her sleep when they served lunch. Candy never noticed the decline of the aircraft or the impact. She died in her sleep.

"Oh no, are we going to die?" Veronica asked with panic in her voice.

"No, of course not," Soraya blurted, holding Veronica's hand tight, "the pilot will have the plane under control soon!"

"I think we're going to die," Madison said and Veronica started to cry.

"No, Madison! We. Are. Not!" Soraya scolded her friend and tried to calm Veronica.

In her seat, Alison stared at the ground between her feet. She wasn't crying and she barely heard the words her friends uttered. She didn't have the same faith as Soraya. Everything wouldn't be okay. They were about to die.

"I love you all," Alison said, as she looked sideways to her friends.

"We love you too," Soraya said and smiled at Alison.

She reached out to touch Alison's hand, but the movement of her arm stopped mid-air the same moment the plane crashed in the desert sand.

Edward realized what was happening just a fraction of a second before Nora did. He saw the panic in her eyes.

"Get down," he said in a firm voice, "grab your ankles."

Nora did as she was told.

Edward tried his best to conceal his own panic. He bent forward too, his head between his knees, and reached for Nora's hand. They were quiet, listening to the panic around them, the screeching engines.

"I love you, my slut," Edward said and tightened his grip on Nora's hand.

"I love you too, Sir."

Those were their last words.

At first, neither Angie nor Harriet understood what was happening. They had both dozed off and woke because of the screams of panic around them. Only seconds later, they realized that the plane seemed to make a nosedive. They had a mutual understanding when they looked at each other and thought: *I'm not ready to die!* Angie and Harriet grabbed each other's hand and both talked at the same time.

"Are we going to die?" Harriet asked.

"I need to tell you something," Angie said.

Then again, they spoke simultaneously, because they both heard what the other had said.

"No, no, we are not!" Angie said.

"Tell me what?" Harriet asked.

Again they understood each other and for a third time they talked at the same time.

"Are you sure?" Harriet asked.

"I'm pregnant," Angie said.

"You're what?" Harriet asked.

"Pregnant."

"But how?"

"Rape. Ten weeks ago."

"The student at the bar? The night I left early?"

Angie nodded.

"But why have you not told me? Why have you not told the police? Oh sweetie, I am so..."

The last thing Harriet did was reaching for Angie to hug her. The impact of the crash threw their bodies in two different directions.

Chapter Sixteen
Identifying the victims

A team of doctors, pathologists and nurses had been assigned to help with the identification of the victims of Flight LU-365 from Amsterdam to Johannesburg. The members of the team came from the Netherlands, South Africa and from Namibia. They asked the residential countries of the victims to send the medical records for each victim, to enable them to identify them. It took the team two weeks to get all medical records from the different countries.

Victims could be identified by their passports, but the team preferred using official identification procedures, which included a postmortem for each of the deceased. The first step in identifying people was taking fingerprints of all victims, where available. Several steps followed, which included the comparison of dental records from the different countries to the records of the deceased, as well as DNA profiling of each victim. For the latter, the team asked for DNA material to be collected from the parents or siblings of the people who had died. Identifying the victims correctly was a lengthy process.

In the meantime, while the team of medical professionals worked round the clock to get the victims identified, the next of kin flew to Namibia to visit the crash site. It became a memorial site, almost a place of pilgrimage. Flowers were everywhere – placed on both sides of the road and out of reach of the high water waves. Parents, siblings, husbands and wives wanted to see where their loved ones died. For a month, family visited the crash site daily, but then the silence of the desert returned again, mixed with the crashing of the waves. Flowers died in the burning sun and drifted away on the wind, bit by bit.

Two months after the crash, the first victims were repatriated to their home countries. The next of kin had the sad tasks to arrange funerals. In some cases the advice was to leave the coffin closed, as the crash had left some of the victims maimed or with severed limbs.

The team of medical professionals identified the last victim five months after the crash.

While families and friends waited for their loved ones to be identified and sent home, several memorial services were held in memory of the victims. People felt the need to talk to others who had lost a loved one. They wanted to share their stories; to tell anecdotes about the deceased. People needed to grief together and to have their sadness understood by others. It eased the waiting for a loved one to be returned.

Chapter Seventeen
Saying goodbye

In the Netherlands, the four friends – Veronica, Soraya, Madison and Alison – were buried on the same day, next to each other. Their husbands opted to have one shared funeral service, because of the friendship of the four women. They wanted them to be united in death too. The funeral service couldn't be done at the funeral home. There wasn't a room big enough to accommodate the family, friends and acquaintances of the four women. The husbands chose to have the funeral service in the theater of the local high school. It was big enough to house five hundred people and on the day of the funeral service, not one seat stayed unoccupied. Family came from all over the country. Members of Soraya's family attended the funeral from Brazil. The service lasted longer than a normal funeral service because of speeches from the husbands, spokespeople of charity organizations and other friends or family members.

Many tears flowed that day. The four women were prominent figures in their town and for one day this town stood still, celebrating their lives and bringing them to their last resting place. At the graveyard, the four coffins stood next to each other, each resting on the bands above an open grave. Family members gathered around the four coffins, standing close to the coffin of their own loved one. Simultaneously the coffins lowered into the ground. Once the closest family had left, people walked by all four of the open graves. Rose petals in four different colors were thrown into the graves and onto the coffins. People paid their last respects before they went home or to the funeral room at the entrance of the graveyard, where they spent time with the families, comforting them and talking about the four women who died in the horrible plane crash.

On the same day of the funeral service of the four friends, the children, grandchildren and friends of Joe and Mattie sat in the funeral home where soft music played. Soon the service preceding the cremation of Joe and Mattie would start. Even though it had been two months since the plane crash, their sorrow was still mixed with disbelief. None of them understood the cruel blow fate had dealt their parents. Mattie and Joe were so happy together. They had been blessed to have a second big love in their lives, only for it to be cut short in such an abrupt and cruel way. The words spoken at their service reflected the disbelief and their sadness. People smiled and wiped away tears when the children of Joe and Mattie brought up anecdotes of their parents. The children pledged to their deceased parents that they would live on as one family, as their parents intended them to be. Music that played in-between the speeches were the favorite pieces of Joe and Mattie – some from their time together and some from before they met. The children, grandchildren and friends sobbed as they walked by the coffins to say their last goodbyes. Some of them stood still for a short while, bowed their heads and moved on. Others touched the coffins as if to touch their father or mother for one last time. The coffins disappeared into the floor, to the basement below, the moment the last people left the room.

In South Africa a group of people stood around an open grave with Table Mountain watching over them. Two coffins stood next to each other, ready to be lowered into the double grave. Kim and Lora were being buried in the same grave. Their parents had discussed this even before their bodies returned to South Africa – they believed that this was what the two inseparable young women would have opted for.

Because of a drizzle people grouped together under umbrellas. The parents of Kim and Lora were quiet. They had no more tears to cry. Fellow students of the two young women attended the funeral too. Some of them knew Kim and Lora from high school and others had attended the same university as the two deceased women. Both fathers spoke a couple of words about their daughters.

"They were always together," Lora's father spoke, "which was a good thing because they could have left behind a trail of broken hearts."

His voice broke when he spoke these words. People smiled and wiped tears from their cheeks. Everyone knew how close Kim and Lora had been. No one suspected exactly how close. Kim and Lora had done a good job of keeping their lesbian relationship a secret.

The pastor said a last prayer at the side of the grave and each person present silently said their last goodbyes. People left and only the parents stayed behind at the grave. Silent. Each with their own thoughts. They held onto their faith in God, believing that Kim and Lora had completed their work on earth and God needed them at His side.

The funerals of Harriet and Angie happened on different days. Angie's body returned home about three months after the crash. Angie's parents had learned that their daughter was pregnant when she died, but they had no idea who the father was. Their shock when they heard about the pregnancy was overshadowed by their grief for her passing. Fellow students of Harriet and Angie attended the funeral. The young man who raped Angie was present too. He was a shadow of what he was on the night of the rape. He had lost weight, had dark circles around his eyes and barely dared to look anyone in the eye. The young student was ashamed of what he had done and wished he had apologized to Angie, even though that wouldn't have taken away what he did. He liked her a lot and when he sobered up the morning after he forced her to have sex, shame kept him from going to her. He constantly put it off; telling himself he would do it the next day and now it was too late. Too late, forever. A month after the cremation of Angie, her ashes were strewn out on the beach, not far from the spot where she was raped several months before.

Harriet's body was one of the last to be repatriated back to her home country. Two months after they had buried their own daughter, Angie's family attended a funeral service again, this time that of Harriet. Just like Angie, Harriet would be cremated. Her parents thought that this was what she would have preferred. Preferences had never been discussed when she was still alive. Their parents hadn't expected their daughter to die before they did. Harriet's lecturer was at her funeral service too. Even though it was five months after the crash and after he had seen her for the last time, he still missed her every day. They had not only been lovers. They were best friends too. He didn't expect to ever find a woman as special as Harriet was. Harriet's parents had never met him. They didn't even know of his existence. He sat alone and talked to no one, isolated in his grief.

Kaitlyn's body came back to the Netherlands four months after the crash. Her husband was incapable of organizing her funeral. He broke down a month after the plane crash and still resided in a psychiatric institution in a near catatonic state. Kaitlyn's husband couldn't forgive himself for letting her go. He believed that she would have left him; that she wanted a divorce. He chastised himself that he should have fought harder to save their marriage. He shouldn't have been so angry with her. She had only tried to rekindle their marriage. He should have listened to her, should have understood that. He believed that if he had been open to her suggestions, she would not have gone to South Africa and would not have died. His thoughts and grief made him withdraw from everyone around him, until Kaitlyn's brother took over and had him admitted to hospital. From there he was transferred to the psychiatric institution.

Kaitlyn's children stayed with her brother, who also took care of the arrangements for her funeral service. He tried to talk to Kaitlyn's husband about whether his sister wanted to be buried or cremated, but in the end he had to decide. He opted for a cremation, hoping that his sister thought about it the same way he did. Friends, family and colleagues paid their last respects as they walked past the coffin and greeted Kaitlyn one last time. One man stopped by the coffin and stood there longer than anyone else had. No one knew who he was. No one heard him whisper the words: "Farewell, my love, my soul mate."

On the same day of Kaitlyn's funeral service, Anthony was buried on the farm of his parents in The Free State, one of the nine South African provinces. The family burial site had been in this location for several generations. The graves of Anthony's great-grandparents and grandparents were there too. He was the first of his generation who would be buried in the small graveyard on the family farm. His parents were devastated about his death.

"This is not how it should be. This isn't right. Parents shouldn't outlive their children," his mother repeated over and over again.

Anthony's two brothers and his sister stood next to the open grave with their spouses and children, as well as Anthony's wife, his children and his parents. They had the funeral service in town, in the only church, but have opted for a burial with only the closest family present. The church was packed with other family, friends of the family and Anthony's colleagues.

Cassidy was in the church too, her red swollen eyes hidden behind sunglasses and her head bowed and hidden under a hat.

The smell of fresh earth filled the air. The minister stood at the head of the grave and read a passage from the Bible, before he said a prayer. Women and children cried. The men tried to comfort the women, doing their best to hide their own tears. Anthony's father had one arm around the shoulders of his wife, the other around the shoulders of Anthony's wife. They watched as the coffin lowered into the grave. It reached the bottom with a thump. Anthony's brothers and father shoveled the fresh earth back into the hole. When they were done, the women and children put flowers on the grave and everyone returned to the farmhouse. The women dabbed their tears. The men hugged and comforted them. As they walked up the stairs, Anthony's mother mumbled the words again: "Parents should not outlive their children."

Chris and Sarah were buried in the graves they had bought back when they just got married, had little money and weren't thinking about dying. They bought the graves because their parents taught them to be sensible and prepared for the future. They laughed when they did it, wondering whether sixty years down the line they would even care where they were laid to rest. Now, a mere twenty-five years after they bought the graves, the holes for their coffins had been dug the day before. In the nearby funeral home, a handful of people gathered for a short funeral service for Chris and Sarah. The couple had always lived sober and sensible and their funeral service reflected that. None of their parents attended the funeral service or burial. Only Sarah's mother was still alive, but she stayed in a nursing home that specialized in dementia. The nurses tried to tell her that her daughter died in a plane crash, to which she replied: "I know no one named Sarah."

Even when they showed her pictures, she couldn't remember that she had a daughter. Neither Chris nor Sarah had siblings. The only people who attended their funeral service were their handful of friends and some of their colleagues.

Just like with Harriet and Angie, the bodies of Brian and Sylvia didn't return home at the same time. Sylvia's body arrived back in the Netherlands a month before Brian's. None of Brian's family attended Sylvia's funeral service, simply because they didn't know who she was. They were aware that he had died with his girlfriend, but their own grief for Brian's death didn't motivate them to look for Sylvia's family. Brian and Sylvia had been together for only two months and never got to the phase where they introduced each other to their parents. Sylvia's funeral service was beautiful. Friends of her sang *'Amazing Grace'* acappella. Tears appeared in many eyes and jaws clenched to stop the sobbing. Friends spoke with fondness about the wonderful friend Sylvia was and family talked about her beautiful and bubbly nature. The service brought as many smiles as it did tears. Everyone paid their last respects, walking by Sylvia's coffin and saying goodbyes in their own way.

Brian's funeral service was attended by his family, but also by his friends in the drug world. They tried to blend in with the rest of the people, but Brian's parents couldn't help to frown on their appearances – the big, flashy cars, the black suits, the cocky attitudes. These people were obviously hardened by life and Brian's parents didn't understand where their son had met them. They shrugged and accepted that these strange people came to pay their last respects to their son. Brian had wanted to be buried. It happened on a rainy, windy day. People clung to their umbrellas, which had no purpose as the wind swept the rain against them. Brian's parents didn't notice. They cried for their son; cried because they needed to say goodbye; cried because they had to leave him out there in the cold, dark grave.

The bodies of Edward and Nora arrived back home on the same day. Their parents had the task to organize their funeral and did it with the help of Nora's sisters. Edward was an only child. On the day of the funeral service, not one empty seat could be found in the funeral home. The parents of Edward and Nora didn't realize that the couple had so many friends. Little did they know that everyone in the kink community who ever had met Edward and Nora, attended the funeral service. Nothing indicated that these people had a different lifestyle. No leather clothes, no chains, no clamps, no cuffs. Close observers would have noticed the jewelry that doubled as collars, rings that symbolized submission or a hint of a tattoo that represented the BDSM symbol. Only insiders knew what to look for and understood what it meant.

Edward and Nora had left a will, in which they stated that they wanted to be buried in the same grave. Their parents honored their wish.

No one claimed Judith's body in South Africa. She had no siblings and her parents had long passed away. Judith had neglected friendships and told none of her former friends about her trip to Europe. No one knew that she died in the horrific plane crash. The authorities contacted Hank, after they found information of him in Judith's house. He refused to talk to them. His new wife knew nothing about the affair he had with Judith and he didn't want her to find out. He didn't see a way to organize Judith's funeral without revealing the nature of their relationship. Judith was given a sober state funeral with only a minister and two government officials present.

Cathy's mom sobbed and wailed during the funeral service. Her husband tried his best to console her, to quiet her down, but to no avail. She was uncontrollable, burying her only child. Her daughter. The daughter she had such big plans for. The daughter she wanted to see married to a wealthy man. The daughter she wanted to dress in a designer's wedding dress. The daughter she had secretly admired because she went her own way, did her own thing and didn't rely on her father's money or connections. The coffin was barely visible under the flower arrangement her parents had put on the coffin. On the floor around the coffin were the bouquets from other family members, friends of Cathy and from her colleagues. In the back, at the far edge of a row sat a young man. Only Cathy's father knew who he was. The young man didn't speak to anyone, but had anyone spoken to him, they would have learned that he came from the country that Cathy was about to visit when the plane crashed. He stayed seated when everyone passed by the coffin to pay their last respects. When everyone had left, he stood up and walked to the coffin. He touched it with the tips of his fingers and whispered: "Goodbye, my love, I will always remember you."

Candy was one of the mutilated victims. A piece of steel from the plane had cut right through her chest towards her shoulder and severed her right arm. The limb had been found and placed in the coffin before it was repatriated back to the Netherlands. On the day of Candy's funeral service, her mother knew who her colleagues were. They were less discreet about their clothes than the members of the kink community at the funeral of Edward and Nora. Candy's mom didn't mind. She had met these people in the months while they waited for Candy's body to come home. They supported her, hugged her when she cried and listened to her when she wanted to talk about Candy. At least once a week, one of them popped in to check on her. They knew she had to do everything alone now, since Candy's father had passed away a month after the plane crash. People said he died of a broken heart. He couldn't bear that his daughter was dead. Candy's colleagues sat in the row behind Candy's mom during the funeral service. Together with her, they were the last to stand at the coffin. The movie director stood next to Candy's mom. He looked at the coffin and said: "She was a star when she lived and now she'll be the brightest star in the sky. A star forever."

Epilogue

The air crash investigation team worked for months to find the cause of the crash of Flight LU-365. They listened to the recordings on the black box, and tried to make sense of every recorded word. They investigated each piece of wreckage, no matter how small or seemingly insignificant. An attack was ruled out and this killed the rumors that went around in the media for good. They ruled out pilot error. Clearing the pilot's name gave his family closure. Weather patterns were checked repeatedly, because sometimes freak weather conditions proved to be the cause of a plane crash.

In the end, they reached the conclusion that the crash probably happened due to a computer malfunction. The plane had stalled mid-air, but according to the computers and dials in the cockpit the plane was still flying with no problems. It was clear from the transcript of the black box that the pilots had checked all the necessary meters and dials and found no signs to explain what was happening to the aircraft.

The investigation on the cause of the computer malfunction continued.